SPARKS
IN THE
DARKNESS

STEVE HIGGS

VINCI
BOOKS

Vinci Books

vinci-books.com

Published by Vinci Books Ltd in 2025

1

A CIP catalogue record for this book is available from the British Library.
Paperback ISBN: 9781036709341

The EU GPSR authorised representative is Logos Europe, 9 rue Nicolas
Poussion, 17000 La Rochelle, France contact@logoseurope.eu

By Steve Higgs

Blue Moon Investigations

A New Entry on the Chart

I had to fight to stop the yawn that was threatening to split my head in two. The phone was ringing, insistently demanding I answer it. Yet even though I could pick it up and thumb the green button to connect the call, there was no way I could speak until I wrestled my fatigue under control.

Worried the caller might ring off if I let it go to voice-mail, I touched the green button anyway.

A second ticked by as the caller waited for someone to speak. My jaw was still wide open, and I considered using both hands to force it shut.

'Hello?' a woman's voice rang through loud and clear. As my yawn finally subsided, I noted the clear, precise nature of the woman's accent. More correctly, I should say that her voice was without an accent, which is to say I heard no regional markers to place her from the west or the north or from a particular county. Rather, she just sounded posh to my ears, her upbringing one that might have involved private schools and Bentleys.

1

I was filling in a lot of blanks with silly imagined scenarios as I fought to get my teeth aligned so I could finally speak.

'Hello?' the woman repeated herself. 'Is there anyone there?'

'Yes, sorry,' I blurted. 'This is Jane Butterworth. Good evening and welcome to the Blue Moon Paranormal Detective Agency. How may I help you?'

'Is this call being recorded?' she asked, the question direct and demanding.

'Um, no,' I lied, turning off the recorder I habitually use.

I heard the woman exhale. 'Very well. My name is Detective Inspector Munroe. I am calling you from Buckingham Palace.'

'Buckingham Palace?' I questioned. 'Where the Queen lives?'

'The Queen is not in residence and rarely stays in Buckingham Palace,' the detective replied matter-of-factly. 'Neither is her majesty a factor in the matter at hand. I require …' the woman fell silent, giving me the impression she was wrestling with how to frame what she wanted to say.

This is not all that unusual in my line of work. As you probably gathered from the title of the firm, we specialise in paranormal investigations. Blue Moon was started by my boss, though I should probably refer to him as my colleague now. I am one of three detectives working at the agency. We have an office on Rochester High Street just a stone's throw from the cathedral. I came to the firm as an assistant to do the general administration tasks. However, after dabbling in a case because there was no one else to tackle it, I was swiftly promoted, and now get my own cases.

Before the police officer could speak again, I tried to

finish her sentence. 'You have unexplainable events at the palace, and you need to hire a specialist who can be quiet and discreet.'

I got to hear DI Munroe sigh with relief. 'Yes, exactly that. Discretion is paramount in this matter.'

'Can you tell me what has occurred?' I begged.

Honestly, I expected her to regale me with a story of a ghost or a mysterious noise in the walls. Given that everything we deal with fell somewhere on the weirdometer, you can imagine how rarely I hear something that surprises me.

However, when she began explaining her problem, I was forced to interrupt. 'I'm sorry, you have a what?' I couldn't help but ask.

'A dragon,' DI Munroe repeated her previous words. 'At least, it flies and breathes fire, and I don't know what else to call it.'

Right. A dragon.

Swapping my phone from right hand to left, I crossed the office to the wall where we have a chart. Tempest – my boss – created it one night as a bit of fun. On the chart are our three names and beneath each are rows which list various creatures. There are ghosts, vampires, werewolves, pixies … you name it, and you can bet someone has called us to investigate one at some point. I was behind on werewolves, failing to score even one case yet, and Amanda was the only one who could claim to have been called to solve an alien-based mystery.

However, I took the handy pen set next to the chart and added a new row, writing the word dragon and putting a big tick under my name.

'Am I correct to assume you would like me to come now?' I checked.

DI Munroe replied instantly. 'Of course, Miss Butter-worth … Is it Miss?' she asked, checking my marital status.

I almost told her that I'm actually a mister, but revealing my true gender when I am dressed and acting as Jane would do me no favours, so I brushed the question to one side.

'Jane will do. I shall leave immediately. How do I gain access to the palace? Is there a way in with my car?'

I listened intently, switching on the recorder again to catch her instructions as she relayed where I needed to go and how to avoid getting shot by the soldiers guarding the palace gates.

With the call ended and my car keys in my hand, I checked the office front door was secure and went out the back. I was going to Buckingham Palace.

Royal Targets

DI Munroe called me before I arrived, anxious to check on my progress. Consequently, she met me at the gate when I revealed I was only a few minutes from arriving. It made getting through the gate easy at least.

'Nice car,' she commented, sliding into the passenger seat of my Aston Martin to guide me through the palace grounds.

'It was a gift,' I admitted. I could never afford to buy such an extravagant car, not least because it was one of the stunt models made for the James Bond Movie, *The Living Daylights*, and still had all the secret buttons and devices on it. Not that the machine guns fired real bullets, they were just props, but it was fun to know I could press a button and have them pop up from the bonnet.

Munroe showed me where to park and started to fill me in on her problem.

'It started more than a week ago.'

'A week?' I questioned, amazed they had let it go on for so long.

5

'I didn't know what it was at the time.' She took a breath and plunged on. 'We found a body. It was one of the soldiers. A young private in the Grenadier Guards by the name of Karl Matthewson. He completed his two-hour watch and was relieved, but failed to return to the guard house. When the soldiers went looking for him, they found his charred remains. He was still clutching his rifle but hadn't managed to get a shot off.'

I stayed silent, noting everything she said in my head because she refused to let me record her or even write anything down.

'I was called at that point. I have quarters in the grounds of the palace,' she explained. 'It was … is my job to investigate, but I will unhappily admit I have no idea what happened to the man. He wasn't near a source of fire, and I am not willing to believe in self-combustion.'

A memory surfaced, jolting me to focus on it. Months ago, we had a case where a man had self-combusted. We investigated on behalf of the family and there were other reports at the time that led us to believe there was a person messing around with fire.

Not your standard arsonist or pyromaniac though, this was something different. This was … magical almost, like there was a person who could create, control, and manipulate fire. The trail went cold, and the case remained unsolved.

So far.

I dragged my thoughts back to the present because DI Munroe was still talking.

'After three days of expert opinion, forensic examination, and painstaking investigation, I had achieved nothing, but then one of the soldiers spotted something inside the palace grounds.'

I kept quiet, desperate to ask questions, but unwilling to interrupt her.

'There was a figure on the roof. Lance Corporal McKinnon's report states that it was a black figure with glowing orange eyes. He also said it had wings, though when I pressed him, he admitted he couldn't be sure about the last part. His words were corroborated by Guardsman Bartlet who was with him. They challenged it and raised the alarm before giving chase. They have a quick reaction force here at all times – it's a standard military thing apparently. The QRF as they call themselves, deployed within seconds, swarming the palace in a bid to cut off the intruder.'

'They didn't catch it,' I supplied, finding myself drawn into her tale.

'No,' she agreed. 'But with pressure from the palace to resolve this issue, and the press sniffing around because the family of the dead soldier are demanding answers, I gave up trying to do this myself and called you.' We were out of my car and walking across the moonlit palace grounds on our way to get inside when DI Munroe abruptly stopped moving.

I turned to face her to find her staring right at me. I guess she felt this part of her story required eye to eye contact so I would know how serious she was.

'The soldiers caught up to the … thing on the roof. It was less than fifty yards from the Queen's bedroom. They opened fire when it disobeyed their challenge and vanished into the shadows. When they saw it again a few seconds later, they resumed firing.'

'They shot it?' I questioned, wondering what I was doing here if the thing they wanted my advice on was already dead.

'The bullets had no effect.' DI Munroe looked scared as

she retold her story. 'According to the after-action report – that's what the soldiers call it – the … dragon smashed through a window and set the curtains on fire, torching the room it went into so the soldiers could not follow.'

I could feel my own pulse rising, the startling nature of this case causing a creeping sense of self-doubt and worry to spread like chilled water through my veins.

'The soldiers were unsure what to do at that point. They never go inside the palace, and I think they hesitated before smashing windows in an adjacent room so they could follow. When they did, they discovered another body, this time one of the palace stewards. He was in the hallway outside the room the dragon broke in through. Wrong place at the wrong time. The QRF fanned out, going room to room as they attempted to find the beast. It was a mercy it didn't get to the members of the royal family currently in residence or … well, you can imagine the headlines if someone broke in and killed the heir to the throne.'

I could indeed, but had a question. 'Who is in residence?'

'Since that second attack, almost no one. There were senior figures here, including the heir to the throne who was in London to host a big event for one of his charities. He was removed to a safer location within hours of the first incursion. Most of the others left shortly thereafter. Only one is still here, Lord Edward Chamberlain, second son of Duke Westborough. The duke is twelfth in line to the throne after Prince Charles, his sons, and Prince Charles' grandchildren. That makes Lord Chamberlain technically fourteenth in line to the throne, but he is far enough down the peerage that he doesn't get any special protection.'

'He is still here despite the attack?' I questioned.

DI Munroe nodded. 'Yes, he's quite cavalier about it

and claims to see no danger. I know the palace wanted him to go but he declined. I am left with the belief he likes being the only royal in residence. Anyway,' she sucked in a deep breath, 'we've been digressing from the topic at hand, and we are yet to get to the best part.'

I cranked an eyebrow, wondering what was going to top the fire breathing dragon.

DI Munroe didn't make me wait. 'I am under orders to sew this up without the press ever knowing about it, but I'm not sure if that is going to be possible.'

'Why not?' I asked, my brow wrinkling with confusion.

DI Munroe pursed her lips and sighed deeply. 'Because of what happened next. The soldiers worked across the palace covering the top two levels in a systematic sweep. They did a great job at enormous personal risk and cornered the *dragon*,' it was clear from the way she said the word that she could scarcely believe it herself, 'as it made its way back to the roof. Then,' she sucked in a deep breath, 'it flew.'

'It flew?'

She nodded. 'That is what more than two dozen soldiers claim. It opened its wings and took off into the night sky. Two of the guardsmen opened fire, their rounds having no effect again. Mercifully, their commander ordered them to cease fire. He was rightly concerned the bullets would come to land in the grounds outside the palace – there are houses nearby and people going past at all times of the day and night.'

I did my best to summarise.

'We have a creature who is bulletproof, able to spew fire, and it can fly. Anything else?'

'Orange eyes,' DI Munroe reminded me. 'They estimated its height at about six feet and described it as able to defy gravity. I don't know what it is, but after the second attack … well, let's just say I am under pressure to prevent a third incident from occurring.'

I watched the detective's face. There was something she wasn't telling me. Something about her personal motivations behind calling a paranormal investigator for help.

'Do you believe it is a dragon?' I sought to clarify.

The detective shrugged. 'I don't know what to think. I can get my head around the bulletproof and the flame thing, but the flying is hard to explain. Whatever my personal thoughts on the matter, my bosses will not entertain the idea that there is a supernatural creature plaguing the palace and if I suggest otherwise, I'll need a new job.'

There it was. That sense of something hidden.

'Why would they take your job away?' I challenged her. She was keeping something secret, and I hated not knowing all the parameters when I go into an investigation. It is like trying to read while looking through gauze.

DI Munroe sucked in a breath as she frowned and was about to give me a dismissive answer when I raised a knowing eyebrow and folded my arms. Her words caught in her throat, and I got to see her shoulders slump.

'It is not germane to the case,' she stated. 'But … look, this is a punishment post for me. You don't need to know the details, but if I don't sew this up quickly, or if I give my boss any just cause to question my ability, he will fire me.'

Enough said. There was something in her past that placed her on a bad footing. She came across as a little desperate and as she started walking again, I fell into step by her side.

It was time to see what clues she might have uncovered.

Two Sides of the Same Team

THURSDAY, OCTOBER 12TH 1934HRS

Inside the palace I got to see the evidence amassed thus far and saw DI Munroe in the light for the first time.

She was five feet and maybe four inches tall, wearing a trouser suit that hid her slender figure and a collared shirt unbuttoned at the top. Her ash-blonde hair was cut into a bob at the same length as her jaw which to me made her head look a bit like a mushroom. I guessed her age to be somewhere in her mid-thirties and she wore no jewellery, not even a ring. Whether she was unmarried or divorced was not a subject I needed to bring up.

She had a large office dedicated to her needs in the basement of the palace. Crime, as you might imagine, was next to non-existent, and I got why she referred to her position as a punishment. It would be hard to shine when there were no crimes to solve and every opportunity to mess up in a high-profile manner if she missed anything that did happen. I was curious to hear what she might have done to earn such a reprimand, but like she said, it was not germane to my visit.

The photographs of the two victims, however, were. They were hard to look at. Behind Guardsman Matthewson's body was a shadow. Or, rather, it was whatever the opposite of a shadow is called. Where the flame hit him, it splayed out to leave a soot mark on the wall and a man shaped hole in the middle of the soot where the wall was mostly untouched.

'Whatever our 'dragon' is using, it burns hot,' remarked DI Munroe, standing next to me as she showed me what she had so far. 'The forensic guys are still analysing it. So far they can tell me what it isn't.'

'What isn't it?'

'A standard accelerant a person can buy off the shelves. Their best guess so far is that it is something organic.'

'Organic,' I repeated her word. 'As in naturally occurring?' Oh, yeah, this was right up there on the weirdometer.

I got a sort of shrug from her – like she said, the boffins were working on it.

A knock on the door preceded a man in uniform entering. He was one of the soldiers, a man in his late twenties with a serious set to his face. He was over six feet tall, and handsome with a nice smile which he turned on me.

'Good evening,' he met my eyes. 'Captain Raef Duncan at your service.' He extended his hand which I shook. I guess something in the back of his head told him my hand was significantly bigger than he expected because his features froze, just for a second, as he looked down at my manly knuckles and back up at my face.

The two things didn't fit.

It's the hardest part of crossdressing and pretending to be a girl. I can change my voice, wear a wig and girl clothes, then use makeup to hide the rest. However, there is just no way to get around the fact that I have size ten feet and man-sized hands.

If Captain Duncan suspected anything, he was astute enough to keep it to himself.

'This is Jane Butterworth,' DI Munroe took care of the introduction. 'She is here to consult on our fiery problem.'

The soldier's serious expression returned.

'You called in outside help?'

'Whatever that thing is, it killed one of your men, Raef. You should be working with me on this.'

The soldier frowned at the detective. 'I am working with you, Cassandra. However, looking for clues and treating this like a criminal act is ridiculous.'

'You think this is a supernatural creature?' I asked, jumping into the conversation.

He swung his face around to pierce me with a dread look. 'I have seen it, Miss Butterworth. I have faced enemy combatants on three continents but never encountered anything I could not explain. I hesitate to call it a dragon, but it flies and breathes fire and has wings. Whatever it is, if it comes back, I intend to catch it or kill it.'

'By shooting it?' questioned DI Munroe. 'Your men tried that already.'

'It was dark, and they were shooting at a fast-moving black target. They missed. That is all.'

The detective wasn't ready to let her point go. 'That is not what their reports claim. They stated that their bullets hit it but had no effect.'

Captain Duncan's features hardened. 'They are mistaken. You can investigate all you want, Cassie. If it invades the palace grounds again, it is my problem to deal with, not yours.'

DI Munroe was becoming visibly annoyed. 'Firing shots inside the palace grounds is just as dangerous as ...'

'As what?' he cut her off. 'As letting a fire breathing creature stalk the palace and burn people to death? It has killed twice already, Detective Inspector.'

While they were arguing, I was gathering my thoughts. I was here and this was supposed to be my area of expertise. Whatever had come into the palace grounds and however it had arrived here, my experience assured me that it was not something paranormal.

Interrupting their increasingly heated discussion, I coughed loudly and started speaking. 'Okay, I want to start by stating that what we are dealing with is a man in a suit.' Neither Munroe nor Duncan saw need to hide their surprise. 'It always is,' I insisted before either could argue. 'The firm I work for specialises in dealing with cases like this and there is never a paranormal explanation. The suit might be high-tech, but it is still a suit.'

'That can fly?' questioned Captain Duncan.

'And spit fire and is bulletproof,' I added. 'Still a suit. My first question is to do with why it is here. Why the palace? This place has an armed squad of soldiers so even if the suit is made of a material that deflects bullets, coming here is an incredible risk. The 'man' must be after something. What do you have of value in the palace?'

Munroe and Duncan both snorted laughs.

'Of value?' questioned Munroe. 'Even the toilet paper is worth a fortune.'

Captain Duncan agreed. 'There are priceless paintings, ornaments, and objects everywhere. Then there is the desire to break into the palace just for bragging rights. For many, just getting to take a selfie inside the palace is enough motive to break in.'

'Hence the palace-assigned senior detective,' pointed out DI Munroe.

I sniffed in a deep breath as I absorbed what should have been obvious to me.

Captain Duncan prompted me to speak. 'Any idea as to what we might be dealing with or how we can stop it?' His tone was mocking.

With both the detective and the senior soldier watching me, I shuffled my feet and gave some thought before speaking. I didn't want to appear flustered or without the ability to provide a clear answer, but that was how I managed to come across.

Before I could answer him, Captain Duncan cut me off. 'Right, good plan. I suspect I could have come up with that by myself.' His response to me taking some time to think was both rude and unnecessary.

'I doubt that attitude will help,' I snapped. 'I arrived a few minutes ago. Do you think perhaps I might be permitted enough time to absorb the information I am presented with?'

The solider snorted a bored laugh. 'Time? Civilians always want time so they can avoid making a decision. We have a *man*, if I accept your belief, in a suit. All I need to do is create an ambush, lure him into my kill box, and end this. We can pick over the why and who of it once he is disabled or dead. If I ignore your looney theory, I then have a creature I cannot explain but it will die just the same when my troops cut it to shreds.'

'You plan to kill him,' I scoffed. 'How is that working out for you so far? Didn't I hear that your bullets have no effect on it? What do you propose to use next? Artillery?'

The captain's features contorted in rage, unhappy to be

spoken down to by a young woman, but when he spoke, he wasn't addressing me.

'There is no need for this … woman to be here, Cassandra. I shall keep this foolishness from my report, but you had better get rid of her now.'

I thought DI Munroe was going to agree with him and that my trip would prove to be wasted, but she rounded on the soldier, glaring up at him.

'You don't tell me what to do, Raef. I'm the palace detective, you're the guard dog.'

Captain Duncan reacted as if slapped, reeling away from the imagined blow only to then bare his teeth. He was about to retort when DI Munroe stopped him.

'I will arrest you if you threaten me,' she stated calmly.

Seething, but holding his tongue, Captain Duncan held back whatever it was he wanted to say. When a couple of seconds had passed and his anger was wrestled under control, he twitched his eyes to me and then back to the police detective.

'My men will bring the creature down. Then we will find out if it is a man or not.' Spinning on his heel, he left no opportunity for argument as he stormed from the room.

'Raef, wait!' DI Munroe called after him. 'Raef, we need to work together.'

His footsteps echoed in the hall outside as he continued unabated. When they faded into the distance, DI Munroe swore.

We were going to get down to business in a second, but before we did there was something I wanted to clear up. I had seen the looks passing between the two of them.

'Did I notice some tension between the two of you?' I asked casually. DI Munroe's eyes had been cast down, but she snapped them up to meet mine now.

'It's that obvious, huh?' She swore under her breath again. 'We dated briefly. I guess I liked the alpha male thing, at least, I did until I got to know him a little better. He's a bully, one of those men who thinks they know what is best for the woman in their life and is prepared to tell them how to behave and ... well, you get the picture. We only slept together once. It has been a problem working with him ever since.'

Now that I had a clear picture and could better understand why he went from reasonable to ridiculous so quickly, I could focus on what needed to be done.

I didn't have a lot to go on and the dragon hadn't been seen for three days. Would it ever return? Was there still a danger to the people in the palace or was there ever? Two people had died but was one of them the intended target or were they both unfortunate victims?

There were a lot more questions than answers and it was time to start picking the detective's brain. I didn't get to do that though because Cassie got a phone call.

A Royal Arrival

I could only hear one half of her conversation, and pretended I wasn't listening as I busied myself going over the meagre evidence.

What was instantly clear from what I did overhear was the arrival of someone unexpected.

When she abruptly ended the call, she tapped me on my shoulder.

'I can't leave you in here or free to roam the palace. Sorry, I need to go so you'll just have to come with me.'

I hooked my handbag with my left hand, scooping it up and onto my shoulder as I went out the door she held open as an unspoken invitation to leave.

Then I followed her, weaving through the corridors in the bowels of the palace. With time to absorb what I had learned and give some thought to how I might tackle the case with a view to resolving the mystery, the first inkling of a plan tickled away deep in my brain.

However, I was feeling quite discombobulated. It was

hard to concentrate on anything because I was in Buckingham Palace.

Actual Buckingham Palace!

Had I known this was how my day was going to turn out, I would have chosen better clothes this morning. Everything I looked at and everywhere I looked, the décor and furnishings were incredible. The paintings on the walls, the walls themselves even and the way the corners at each doorway were carved and infilled with gold leaf would look ridiculous anywhere else, but here it just made the place look like a palace.

My eyes were out on stalks constantly.

It made me wish I was wearing a ballgown or a really sharp business suit. Instead, I had gone with skinny white jeans, caramel leather ankle boots with a low, chunky heel, a thick knitted sweater over a silk vest and a leather jacket that matched my boots. I felt very much underdressed.

'Lord Chamberlain,' DI Munroe called as we came into a large hall.

My belly did a little flip flop when a man turned to look our way. Was I supposed to bow or something?

The man was just taking off his coat. There was moisture on it to let us know it was raining outside. I wondered how long it might last.

Lord Chamberlain was short and a little scruffy. I judged his age to be early thirties though he looked older due to a receding hairline which made his skull look like it had forced its way through his hair to emerge on top. His chin was weak, he didn't stand straight, and his eyes were watery.

There were two men in palace livery behind him and half a dozen large cases piled two high – his luggage I guessed. I couldn't fill that many cases if I packed everything I owned.

'Ah, Detective Inspector. Lovely to see you. How are things at the palace?'

She didn't bow when she reached him, so I didn't either, falling in behind and to her left where I remained silent and hoped I wouldn't be noticed.

'Were you expected, Lord Chamberlain?' she asked. 'I was not informed.'

'Why would you be informed?' boomed a deep voice from our left. Another man was coming down a short flight of steps to join us and he bore a stern expression. In his late sixties or maybe slightly older, he wore a fine tweed suit and waistcoat with a chain for a pocket watch. His tie ... I couldn't be certain, but I was willing to bet it was from a military regiment.

'Sir Cuthbert!' exclaimed Lord Chamberlain in the same manner one might when seeing a favourite relative.

DI Munroe leaned her head across to whisper, 'Lord Cuthbert is the head of the palace staff.'

Sir Cuthbert came to a stop a few feet away, addressing the royal family member warmly before turning his attention to Cassie.

'Should you not be engaged in your investigation, Detective Inspector?' he posed the question in a rhetorical manner. 'Perhaps I should speak with the commissioner and see if he can motivate you to do your job.' There was a story there and I was beginning to feel that I needed to know what it was even if she did not wish to share it with me.

With a calm voice, though I could feel the tension radiating off, her DI Munroe replied.

'Sir Cuthbert, I am doing my job, but it is made far more complex when I do not know who is staying in the palace.'

'This is not a planned visit,' Lord Chamberlain interjected with a smile. 'My brother, Eddie, sent for me. I've no idea what it might be about. Probably something to do with papa.'

If I had it right, I was looking at the elder Lord Chamberlain. DI Munroe named the only royal in residence as Edward and said that he was the younger of two sons of the Duke of Westborough.

Whether I was right about the relationship between the two brothers was something I was going to have to ask about later because Lord Chamberlain's gaze was firmly locked on me.

'And who is this fine young filly?' he guffawed lecherously. 'A newcomer to the palace. Perhaps I should show you around my family's humble abode, eh? I bet you and I could find a way to while away the evening.'

My jaw dropped open, baffled by what the correct response in such a situation might be. He was hitting on me in front of DI Munroe and Sir Cuthbert and openly propositioning me with … what? Sex? That was how it sounded.

'This is Jane Butterworth, sir.' DI Munroe introduced me. 'She is here to deal with the *incident* we had last week.'

'Yes, yes. I heard about that. Some kind of break in and a fire, Eddie said. Terrible business.'

'You will be staying the night?' DI Munroe enquired.

Lord Chamberlain shot her a cheeky smile. 'Saucy.'

Munroe sighed and rolled her eyes. I was coming to understand that his flirting was automatic and continuous just as much as it was unwelcome and pointless. Even if he was gay and I was single, I would rather chew my arm off than spend time in the loathsome man's company.

Sir Cuthbert's gaze was fixed firmly on Cassie and me, his unspoken instruction quite clear – go away.

'If you will excuse us, Lord Chamberlain,' DI Munroe ignored Sir Cuthbert and spoke only to the royal family member. 'We have duties to which we must attend.' DI Munroe backed up, bumping against my arm as a signal to turn around and go the other way.

I did just that, but in so doing also took my eyes off the member of the peerage – the first I had ever met – and thus lowered my guard.

'Aaah!' I cried in surprise when he pinched my bottom. Caught out by his unexpected move, I forgot to use my *Jane* voice and now everyone was looking at me.

Blushing, and making sure to employ the correct voice, I snapped, 'Keep your hands to yourself.'

DI Munroe, still frowning and uncertain what she should make of the deeper voice she just heard, nevertheless agreed with me.

'Yes, sir. That was sexual assault, sir. Be warned.'

He didn't like being told off but raised his hands in surrender as we walked away.

I expected the police detective to ask outright if I was a girl or a boy when we got around the corner, but the subject she went with was the presence of the additional royal.

'I don't like it,' she revealed quietly. 'I don't like that his brother refused to leave, but now he is inviting family members here to join him?'

We had ascended to ground level to intercept Lord Chamberlain because DI Munroe wanted to know why he had chosen to visit. Heading back to her office, we were about to descend a staircase when shadows shot by outside and we both heard shouting.

A Crazy Plan

In the space of a heartbeat, we were running. I had to follow the detective – the palace is a maze, and I might never have found a door without her to guide me.

I was shocked to see her produce a weapon. It came from somewhere inside her jacket, a small handgun – what type I could not tell you – but it fit snugly into her tiny hand as she held it down to her right side and ran for the door.

We burst into the garden at the back of Buckingham Palace where a huge lawn stretched out towards tall trees. Moonlight, peeking between clouds, reflected off a distant lake. The rain had stopped, just about, but the fresh scent one always gets after the rain lingered.

My heart was banging in my chest, adrenalin pumping through my veins as I skidded to a stop on the wet flagstones outside.

Half a second was all it took to assess what we were seeing. The soldiers were running through some drills.

There was no danger, that was the first thing to take away. The uniformed men, wearing combat fatigues rather

23

than the impressive red tunics with the bearskin hats, were dashing here and there, but doing so in a controlled, not panicked or urgent manner.

DI Munroe muttered something I couldn't catch, her words not intended for anyone to hear probably, and she turned around to go back inside.

'This dragon case has given me the jitters,' she complained. 'Raef regularly has them performing exercises. Until recently, I think they all considered it a waste of time – the palace was never going to be attacked. I guess now his soldiers must accept he was right to ensure they were ready. At least with them outside, if the dragon comes back, they will be able to repel it.'

'Yeah, about that,' I started, letting the teasing sentence get her attention. 'Maybe we shouldn't go all out to scare it away when it comes back.'

DI Munroe offered me an expression that questioned my sanity.

'What are you proposing? We leave the door open and invite it inside?'

'Shooting it out of the sky is fraught with danger because the bullets will fall to earth in a populated area,' I reminded her. 'Plus, it seems impervious to the injuries inflicted. If you cannot shoot it down, perhaps we should be looking at alternative ways to stop it.'

'Such as?' she encouraged me to expand.

I drew in a deep breath and laid out my idea. When I finished, Cassie – she got bored with me calling her detective inspector the whole time and invited the use of her first name – took her time responding.

When she did, I could see she was trying to find the right words. 'That is probably the craziest plan I have ever heard.' I was going to have to convince her. 'But,' she held up a hand to stop me talking, 'it could actually work. It's not as if I have a better plan myself.'

There were a few problems with cases like this one. A crime occurred that defied explanation, but we like those at Blue Moon because it is where we come in. Tempest taught me to look at things differently from how others might and by doing so we solve most of the cases we get.

It takes a while though. If there is no continued threat, that is not too much of a problem, but the flying, bullet-proof, fire-spitting apparition at the centre of this case could return at any time.

It raised the stakes and I wanted to set a trap to catch it. However, we could not calculate how long it would be before it returned. It could be in five days or five minutes so my daft idea might bear fruit, but there was no telling when.

To that end we would set it up, but then Cassie was going to have to employ people to monitor it.

Since she was in agreement, I posed the next obvious question. 'So, where do we get a net?'

The Younger Brother

The answer was closer than I expected. The soldiers had an indoor five-a-side court with goals at each end. Cassie was convinced we were more likely to run into trouble from the soldiers when they found out than we were from the dragon if it returned.

Watching for the guardsmen, we snuck across the palace grounds to get to their recreation area. My plan, daft as it sounds, was to leave a window open and invite the dragon into the palace. Cassie didn't want it inside, but under pressure to find out who was behind it, and willing to admit she had no faith in the soldiers' ability to catch it or shoot it down, she was willing to try anything.

It would all be arbitrary if the dragon didn't come back.

Cassie led a winding route to get to where she wanted to go – avoiding the soldiers she explained. They were easy to avoid because they never set foot inside the residential areas of the palace. She didn't, as a rule, but was free to go where she needed within reason.

Explaining as she went, I learned most of the soldiers

who chased the dragon three nights ago had entered the palace proper for the first time. They didn't live within the grounds but came in for their rotation of guard duty, typically lasting twenty-four hours, then went home or back to their barracks again. The ceremonial duty – the very public guardsmen photographed by thousands of tourists a day – was considered an honour, but not one that required them to enter the palace.

They had a guard house at the back of the grounds where it was tucked away from visitors' eyes and a small recreational area so they could exercise in their downtime. If they fancied a kick about tonight, they were going to discover their goal nets had been requisitioned.

The nets proved unwieldy and cumbersome. Even balled up carefully so we could carry them, they were heavier than I had anticipated, and bits kept slipping from my hands to snag my feet which I couldn't see with my arms full.

Grunting and panting, I stopped on a landing for Cassie to catch up and tell me which way I now needed to go.

'Hello,' said a voice from behind me.

I turned to find a man eyeing me curiously. He wore slouchy grey cotton jogging bottoms and had bare feet. His top half was covered by a faded Hackett polo shirt. Cradled under his left arm, a small brown sausage dog slept with his head on his owner's forearm. The man had a mug of steaming tea in his right hand, the string of the teabag looped around the mug's handle.

He was in his late twenties, making him a few years older than me, but goodness he was handsome. I took in his features and proportions, observing the small stain on his shirt where food had dropped, and the marks on his thumbs where his uncalloused hands had been rubbed raw.

27

You've got a boyfriend. The words echoed in my head, reminding me that I wasn't supposed to be dribbling at the man-candy somehow making grubby casual wear look good. The thin waist and wide shoulders were complemented by a strong jaw and dazzling blue eyes.

Eyeing me critically, he took a sip from his mug before saying. 'I do not recall seeing you before. I would shake your hand, but you appear to have them both full. I'm Eddie.'

I gulped, trying to find my voice as I shuffled the net to get a hand free.

'I'm Jane,' I squeaked, losing control of the stupid net, and dropping it. The net didn't want to be dropped though, opting as a sign of its displeasure to snag the handbag I'd looped around my neck to keep my hands free.

It pulled my head down, causing Eddie to dart forward and rescue me.

'Here, let me take that,' he offered, scooping the goal net effortlessly while handing me his mug to hold. 'Where are we going with it, Jane?' he smiled in a way that made my tummy tighten.

'The western terrace,' puffed Cassie, finally broaching the top step to arrive on the landing too. Seeing then who had asked the question, she inclined her head. 'Lord Chamberlain.'

'Detective Inspector Munroe, good evening. Might I enquire as to what you ladies are up to? It seems you have a devilish plan afoot.'

Cassie blew him off with a casual dismissal. 'Nothing exciting, I can assure you, sir.'

He wasn't fooled. 'Really? It looks to me like you are planning to net our fiery friend if he makes another appearance.'

Switching topics, quite deliberately I felt sure, Cassie asked him, 'Did your brother find you, sir?'

Lord Edward Chamberlain's features froze, just for a second. 'Find me?'

'Yes, sir,' replied Cassie. 'He arrived half an hour ago. He claimed you invited him, sir.'

'I hardly think so,' replied Lord Chamberlain with a scoffing tone. 'Nugent has no time for his little brother. He hasn't had a civil word for me in years.'

'Why is that?' I asked without thinking, my cheeks colouring when the royal swung his gorgeous gaze my way. Was it too late to add a 'sir' now?

If I had just insulted him by addressing him as if we were equals, the member of the peerage didn't seem to notice.

'Father favoured me,' Edward revealed. 'He always did since I was born. Ever since I came along and stole father's attention away from a young boy, my elder brother has hated me for it. I doubt it helps that my brother ...' he struggled to complete the rest of the sentence and I wondered what he might have been about to say when he added, 'Well, I don't think Nugent is happy that he lost his hair so young and mine appears to be going nowhere.'

Edward had been looking for a way to modestly point out how vastly different the brothers were. Coming from the same genetic soup, they could not be more different. Where the elder brother and heir to the Dukedom (is that the right term?) had a weak chin, poor posture, and no hair, his brother looked like an Italian aftershave model.

'He's in the palace, is he?' Lord Chamberlain sought to confirm.

'Indeed, sir,' replied Cassie. 'Perhaps he is looking for you.'

I was curious to learn why the elder lord might visit if his younger brother had not invited him. If they got along so badly, why visit at all? It was all a little bizarre and was making my Spidey senses tingle.

'I shall look for him once I have helped you ladies get to where it is you are going.'

'No need, sir,' argued Cassie. 'We can manage.'

'No doubt,' he agreed with a smile. 'But I am nothing but a lazy royal with too little to occupy my time. Some exercise will do me good.' He plopped his dog on the carpet. 'You can get some exercise too, Henkel.' While his dog stretched and arched his back, Lord Edward scooped my net under one arm, and Cassie's under the other, before suggesting she should, 'Lead on.'

In a bedroom at the back of the palace where it overlooked the garden and the lake beyond, Cassie opened a window to let in the cold night air.

'The trap will be here?' asked Lord Chamberlain, nodding his head as if he could envisage the dragon becoming ensnared.

'Perhaps, sir,' Cassie was attempting to shoo the royal member away. 'Thank you for your help. Miss Butterworth and I will take it from here.'

'But I can help,' he protested. I couldn't tell, but wondered if he was bored and in need of something to do or trying to find a legitimate reason not to find his brother.

'Police business, sir,' argued the detective inspector.

Lord Chamberlain or Eddie, as I had come to mentally label him, backed away with his hands up and a broad smile showing off his perfect teeth.

'Yes, quite right, I'm sure. Don't want the inbred royal mucking things up.' He shot me a smile and a wink. Eddie, fourteenth in line for the crown was self-deprecating and modest. That he was willing to make jokes about himself and act the fool made me feel yet more drawn to him.

He backed away to the door, made a show of bowing before he left the room and vacated it with a final wish for good luck and good hunting.

I watched the empty space in the doorway for a few more seconds before turning my attention back to the task at hand.

The nets were bundled on the carpet in two piles. Somehow we two girls had to erect them in such a way that they would ensnare the dragon if it came into the room.

A cold breeze blew through the open window making me wish I had picked a thicker coat. Cassie felt it too and it gave urgency to our movements, both to keep us warm and to get the job done so we could go somewhere that was less breezy.

I closed the bedroom door and picked up one of the nets. This was my daft idea – I needed to be the one to present a solution.

Outside in the dark we could hear Raef's soldiers dashing to-and-fro. I didn't want to think of them as trigger-happy fools, but their guns scared me. Shooting at the dragon achieved nothing in their previous attempts. What did Captain Duncan think they would gain from repeating the same thing?

If they were shooting at it, I wanted to be nowhere near them.

Reusing the ornate cord intended to tie the curtains back, the windows themselves, once opened inwards, plus a great deal of puffing, panting, and the use of rude words, we got one of the nets erected. It hung in such a manner that should the dragon come through the window, it would hit the net and be instantly ensnared.

That was the idea. How well it might work and what we did then was anyone's guess. Standing back, Cassie admitted she was impressed.

'It's better than anything I might have come up with,' she conceded. 'Let's put the other one up in a different room.'

We did precisely that, grunting, straining, and balancing on chairs to reach high enough, but ten more minutes of work gave us a second trap.

Taking my hand for balance as she stepped down to the floor, Cassie remarked, 'I guess all we can do now is wait.'

I nodded. 'Let's not wait here though. It's cold.' My fingers were going numb from the cool air spilling through the open window.

'Tea?' suggested the detective. She was rubbing her hands together and blowing on them, the air in front of her face a billowing cloud as her breath hit the cold.

But here's the thing about setting a trap – you need to then watch it. Only once we left the cold and drafty bedroom on a mission to get mugs of hot tea did it occur to me that should the dragon make an appearance we had no way of knowing about it.

'Oh, bother,' I commented when Cassie pointed out my thoroughly obvious mistake. By then we were halfway back to her office in the bowels of the palace. 'I need to go back.'

'I'll go,' Cassie volunteered. 'You get the teas.'

I was about to suggest we trade jobs because I wasn't sure I could find my way to her office by myself and certain I would never find my way back to the bedrooms with the traps in. It was probably easy once a person became better acquainted with the palace, but to me it all looked the same. None of that left my mouth though, because the air filled with the sound of gunfire.

Fire

THURSDAY, OCTOBER 12TH 2048HRS

When the shooting started, there was a heartbeat of indecision where we both looked at each other, and then, without either one of us saying anything, we were running.

If the dragon was here – I couldn't imagine what else the troops were firing at – it meant right now was our best hope for the trap to work. Would it see the open windows? We left table lamps on, rather than each bedroom's main lights. They cast enough light to show the easy access point but not so much that the presence of the nets would be obvious.

Or so we hoped.

Racing up a flight of stairs to get back to the next floor, my pulse was through the ceiling. I had to tell myself that whatever we were dealing with, it was not a mythical or supernatural creature. It wasn't a demon or a fire-breathing dragon or anything else, even if the eyewitness reports suggested otherwise.

As further proof that I hadn't really thought through my

plan, it dawned on me that if we burst through the bedroom doors and found the dragon trapped by our net, it would probably still be able to breathe fire. Not only did we have nothing with which to subdue it, we had no protection against the flames. Even St George thought to take a shield with him!

No sooner had my latest worry registered in my brain than DI Munroe reminded me that she was armed. She yanked her gun from its holster as we got to the bedroom door and shoulder-barged into the room with the weapon pointing at the window.

I ran in after her giving little thought to my own safety. I wanted to see if we had been successful.

The net, however, was still in place.

Cassie yelled, 'The other room!' and spun about to go back out. I blocked her path and needed to get my own body facing the other way. Before I could, I saw the look in her eyes.

It was raw terror.

She wasn't looking at me. Her eyes were aimed above my head to where the ceiling met the wall and twisting around to follow her horrified gaze, I found out what had her so scared.

Hovering in the air just above the door we needed to escape through was a black apparition. Hidden in the shadows, but easy to see nevertheless because its bright orange eyes were glaring down at us, the dragon slowly beat its wings.

Its wingspan was as wide as the body and legs were long. Even though the room was lit, the small table lamps cast shadows and it was hard to make out fine detail. The one thing that registered in my terrified mind was that its proportions were that of a human.

My brain felt disconnected from the rest of me. I could not explain what I was looking at, but it was flying, and it had us trapped. My knees wanted to fold out from underneath me and I questioned whether there would be anything left of my remains other than a sooty mess.

A second ticked by, no one moving until I felt Cassie grabbing hold of my shoulder. She was shouting something, but my eyes were locked on the dragon's featureless face. The orange eyes made it hard to see any other part of the dragon so all I had was an impression of wingspan and the black scales covering its body.

Until the flame appeared.

At the same time, from the corner of my eye I spotted Cassie's gun rising. Her grip on my shoulder was tugging me backward and what she had shouted a second ago finally sunk into my head.

'Window!'

Her gun went off, a thunderous boom that was so close to my face it seemed to shake the fillings in my teeth. I was twisting, trying to keep my balance as she yanked at my clothing. The open window was right there. It didn't offer much as a means of escape and the fall to the ground had to be at least fifty feet.

We might not survive hitting the ground, but the expanding flame behind me as the dragon started to spew fire left me no choice but to find out.

The gun went off again. I hadn't seen either shot land but since the dragon wasn't down or showing signs of wanting to give up, whether Cassie hit it or not mattered little.

We ducked under the bottom edge of the net roughly four feet off the ground and as I felt the wall of heat making the air behind me blister, the pair of us dove through the hole in the wall and into the night beyond.

Flame shot over our heads searing my lungs with its heat. The light accompanying it was so bright I lost my vision. Was that a mercy? I wouldn't see the ground coming at me. I would just hit it and that would be that. Much better than getting cooked extra crispy.

How long would it take to fall fifty feet? The answer, it turned out before my eyesight returned, was far shorter than I could have imagined.

The air whooshed from my lungs as I slammed into gravel with my chest. It hurt, but rolling to a stop with my senses reeling, I knew I had something wrong.

'Come on!' screamed Cassie, firing her gun again. Her hand found my arm, gripping the flesh around my bicep so hard it must have bruised as she pulled me to get up.

The bright light in my eyes was fading, leaving a corona behind, but I could see now that the ground we hit was less than four feet beneath the level of the window.

There was a balcony or parapet running along outside! The correct term for it mattered not one jot. The point is, I hadn't seen it in the dark earlier. Too focused on erecting the net, and deliberately not looking down as I balanced near the window, I just didn't spot that it was there.

Getting dragged along by Cassie, I stumbled and almost fell. She was getting away from the window. The curtains inside were ablaze, so too the net from the football goal which was now the thing stopping the dragon from following us.

I saw its black shape illuminated by the dancing flames as I ran beside Cassie. She had a radio in her hand, but the message she needed to pass was already out there – the palace is on fire, and the dragon is inside.

We stopped running, facing back the way we came when we reached the extent of the balcony. We were two or more rooms along from the one now filled with fire and gasping for breath.

Neither one of us said anything until Raef's voice screeched over the airwaves.

'What did you do? You let it in, you idiot!'

DI Munroe swore loudly and lifted the radio back to her mouth.

'Send your QRF to the west wing, Captain Duncan. They have a fire to fight. There is an intruder in the palace, evacuate everyone to the basement level. I will find the Lords Chamberlain.'

'You'll do nothing!' snapped Captain Duncan. 'I am in command here. You have done enough. Return to your quarters and stay out of our way. Out.'

The radio clicked off, Captain Duncan ending his conversation with the detective in a manner that left little room for argument.

Cassie swore again.

'Is that right?' I asked, still trying to get my breath back. My chest hurt where I slammed it into the gravel, and I felt certain I was going to need a few Band-Aids to deal with the cuts and grazes. My clothes were ruined too, changing my stance on wishing I had worn my best outfit, but I was upright and able to function. 'Is he in charge?'

'Yes,' Cassie spat between tight lips. 'There is an intruder in the palace and threat to life. This is all his jurisdiction.'

'What does that mean for you?' I managed to ask between laboured breaths. 'Are you in trouble?'

'I don't care,' she growled, her words aimed at herself more than me I thought. 'I need to get inside and make sure that ... *thing* doesn't hurt anyone. God, I am such an idiot! I practically invited it inside.'

Without another word, she lined up her gun and fired into the nearest window. I was about to ask what the heck she was doing, but the answer was obvious; she had shot out the locking mechanism on the inside and was now forcing the window open.

The net and the open windows had been my idea. I knew that would matter little when they came to account for what had happened. Detective Inspector Munroe invited me here, so everything thereafter was on her. I parked the guilt I felt building in my gut and climbed through the open window after her.

A stampede of footsteps heralded soldiers arriving in the hallway outside. When we emerged from the bedroom, half a dozen twitchy guns swung our way. It was enough to make me cry out in alarm.

There were thirty or more of the quick-reaction force filling the hallway. Some had their guns pointing this way and that, their non-commissioned officers shouting orders. Others had their rifles slung across their backs as they carried firehoses.

They were tackling the fire and their swift reactions would wrestle it under control before it could spread from the room in which it started, but the door to that room was open and the dragon was somewhere else now.

Amid the deafening noise of high-pressure water dousing the flames and the continued shouting of soldiers giving orders, the sound of Captain Duncan's voice still reached my ears.

'I told you to leave the area!' he shouted, weaving through the men filling the corridor.

Sir Cuthbert appeared, halting Raef's progress with a hand. I had to move position to see where he had come from, spotting a set of stairs I had not noticed before. They were narrow and lacking the sweeping architectural notes I saw everywhere else.

'Sir Cuthbert again,' swore Cassie.

'What's his role here?' I asked. It hadn't been pertinent before, but he was getting involved now.

Cassie spat, 'He's an officious interfering old busybody. However, his official title is Master of the Palace. His word is law here.'

'Captain Duncan, kindly explain yourself,' Sir Cuthbert demanded. 'What on earth is happening here? I heard Detective Inspector Munroe claim there is an intruder in the palace!'

'That's right,' snarled the captain, his eyes not on the man in the suit, but aimed firmly at Cassie. 'She let him in,' he pointed an accusing hand in our direction. 'The woman with her, if that is what she is,' he added snidely, 'is some daft paranormal investigator. Unable to solve this case herself, Detective Inspector Munroe is clutching at straws and willing to turn to any charlatan trickster who claims to be able to help.'

'A paranormal investigator?' the master of the palace repeated disbelievingly, his tone dripping with derision and horror as he turned to see where the senior soldier's hand pointed. 'What the devil …'

'Exactly, Sir Cuthbert, exactly. She's completely lost the plot, and this fire is the result. Rest assured my men have it under control. It will not spread. We are sweeping the upper galleries now, attempting to find the intruder.'

Both men were glaring at me and Cassie with utter

STEVE HIGGS

contempt. I had a dozen responses lined up but couldn't tell if speaking my mind would make things better or worse for the detective.

I never got to find out, because a shout rang out.

'It's on the roof!'

Fire at Will

THURSDAY, OCTOBER 12TH 2055HRS

The cry came from inside the torched bedroom. One of the soldiers checking the blaze was properly out – the fire brigade would be along soon to check their handiwork, I felt certain – had seen something through the open window.

His colleagues, dropping their fire-fighting equipment, were running to his side to get a look too.

I was about to follow, my right foot just starting to lift from the carpet when I heard a terrible cry of alarm.

'Help me! Someone help me! There's a dragon!' The voice was unmistakably that of Lord Edward Chamberlain, the handsome youngest son of a duke.

I was not the only one who heard it.

Cassie and Captain Duncan banged into each other as they both rushed to get into the destroyed bedroom. Water dripped from every surface, and the carpet squelched beneath my feet as I raced to get a look for myself.

Taller than Cassie, and indeed many of the soldiers with my heels to add a few inches, I could see over their heads.

All eyes were trained on the rooftop adjacent to us and two stories above.

Where the rear façade of the palace was anything but a flat face, the portion we were looking at jutted out into the rear gardens. High up on the parapet, Eddie ran for his life. I could see something in his hands, his little dog, Henkel, no doubt.

Holding the dog as he ran was slowing him down, preventing the peer from pumping his arms, and he really needed to go faster because the dragon was coming right for him.

The black shape swooped down over the palace rooftop, coming from high in the night sky and only visible because it created an even blacker spot in the darkness. Until the flame appeared in its mouth again, that is.

'A man in a suit, is it?' screamed Raef, shoving me roughly to one side. He had no further words for me and wasn't hanging around to hear my reply. 'Out the window, all of you!' he commanded his men. 'Two fire teams. Corporal Bates take five men to the south corner and stay out of sight until you hear my shout. We are going to drive it to you! When I give the command, unleash hell!'

The soldiers scrambled to get out of the window, hastily obeying Raef's orders. Shunted aside and ignored, I could hear them making their weapons ready.

'Fire!' bellowed Captain Duncan, his order resulting in a deafening cacophony of shots as the soldiers attempted to shoot the black apparition from the air.

I couldn't hope to estimate how many shots were fired by the dozen or more soldiers to Raef's left and right, but more than a hundred easily.

Cassie was screaming something, her voice hopelessly drowned out by the gunfire.

Eddie vanished around the side of the roof, running for all he was worth just as a gout of flame shot from the dragon's mouth. It lit the night sky. Like a lance of bright light, it beat the darkness into submission and burned my eyesight for a half second.

In that moment of bright illumination, I saw bullets strike the dark form of the dragon all along its flank. The guardsmen were accurate, but the wounds they inflicted made no difference to the creature.

The flame and its searing brightness were gone no sooner than they appeared but having looked at it, any hope of picking out the dragon against the dark sky was gone.

The soldiers were still shooting at the spot where it had been and perhaps it was still there though I couldn't see it at all.

Cassie slammed into Captain Duncan, knocking his trigger finger away and sending him sprawling into the soldiers to his left.

'Cease fire, you idiot!' she screamed into his face. 'Where are those bullets landing? You've no idea, man! Fire another shot and I'll arrest you myself!'

Her actions had the desired effect, the shooting petered out in the next second as the soldiers turned their attention to their commander.

Grunting and growling in his anger and disbelief, Raef pushed himself off the ground. I thought he might attempt to strike the detective, but what he did was much worse. He pointed his rifle directly at her face.

'Get in the way again, Munroe, and I will have you bound and gagged. This is your mess, and I am going to fix it. Protecting the royal family and the palace is my job.'

'You almost shot Lord Edward,' Cassie spat, paying no attention to the muzzle of the gun hovering a foot in front of her eyes. 'Your shots are having no impact on the dragon, and you are endangering life. When this is over, I will arrest you for threatening me. Are we clear on that?' She was speaking through gritted teeth, rage bubbling beneath the surface, but being kept in check by an iron will.

A voice from behind her said, 'Captain Duncan is in command here, Detective Inspector Munroe.' I turned to find the Master of the Palace, Sir Cuthbert, coming to Raef's side. Ignoring Cassie, he spoke over her head. 'Carry on, Captain Duncan. Take down that beast at all costs.'

I could see Cassie fuming. She was the sole voice of reason – no one was going to pay any attention to me – and she had no ability to influence events.

'Where did it go?' demanded Captain Duncan, turning back to his troops. 'Can anyone see the target?' His words were urgent yet controlled – he wasn't panicking and even if he felt fear, he was doing a great job of hiding it. If anything, I believed he was revelling in the action and drama.

No one could spot where the dragon might have gone, but to me that just meant it was still chasing Eddie and they were both out of sight on the other side of the roof.

Outside, on the gravel covering the parapet, the soldiers were taking off across the palace. They wanted to have a clear shot if the dragon reappeared, and they were running to get to where they last saw it. That would require climbing two floors, but the sound of their boots was already fading, only their officer's loud commands echoing in the night air remained to tell us where they were.

Cassie grabbed my arm, yanking me with her as she ran for the door and the interior of the palace.

'That trigger happy idiot is as likely to kill Lord Edward as save him!'

Sir Cuthbert stepped into her path.

'Detective Inspector Munroe, I believe you should return to your office and wait there. I shall be speaking with your superiors shortly and expect a full report on my desk within the hour. Destruction of palace property is not taken lightly, you know.'

I wondered how the already irate police officer might react to the officious man and got my answer in a spectacular fashion.

'Get out of my way, you old fool!' she placed a stiff hand on his shoulder to push him backward from the room and out in the hallway beyond. 'Do something useful and make sure there are no palace staff in the open. Find everyone you can and get to the basement. Then stay there!'

Much like Captain Duncan had with us, she then dismissed him, uninterested to hear what he might have to say in reply to her instructions.

A volley of shots rang out, the distant sound of men shouting back and forth easy to make out through the thick walls of the palace.

'Where are we going?' I shouted, racing after Cassie as she sprinted down the hallway.

Running as hard as she could, her answer came back as a shout between hard breaths, 'My priority is to keep the family safe! Lord Edward is in trouble, and we must get to him. First, though, I need to check Lord Nugent. He's on the next floor and chances are he's still in his room!'

I was out of breath before we got to the stairs and gasping to get enough air in by the time we had raced up them to the next floor. My lungs were searing but I ran on, chasing after the older, yet fitter police officer and reminded myself, not for the first time, that I needed to visit the gym more regularly.

The palace detective ran like a woman with a mission, ripping along the hallway until she skidded to a halt. She had been going so fast, she almost went past the door she wanted and had to grab hold of the door frame to arrest her forward motion.

Too close on her heels to adjust my trajectory, I collided with her. Mercifully, we stayed upright, Cassie's grip on the doorframe enough to stop me too.

Shaking me off, she slammed the door open, her left shoulder leading as we burst into what I guessed would be Lord Nugent's rooms.

The sight that met our eyes rooted us both to the spot.

Evidence

Strewn across the carpet were electronic components and pieces of carbon fibre frame like one might find on a high-end bicycle. To my right, I spotted a small barrel. It was silver in colour and bore a warning symbol to tell everyone the contents were highly flammable.

On a couch dead ahead were pieces of black material. I made to move forward, desperately curious to get a closer look but found my way barred by Cassie's arm.

'Touch nothing,' she hissed, her voice quiet as if we might disturb someone.

The obvious conclusion we were both drawing was that Lord Nugent, freshly returned to the palace, was the dragon. Quite how and why was beyond me to fathom yet, but if the creature we saw was a man in a suit, what I could see spread out around the room were the pieces used in its manufacture.

The detective took out her phone and started taking pictures.

We were both breathing heavily and had made enough

47

noise arriving in Lord Nugent's chambers that we could be fairly certain he wasn't here. Nevertheless, Cassie called out to be sure.

'Lord Chamberlain? Lord Nugent, are you here?'

When no answer came back, Cassie set off to check the rest of his suite of rooms.

'Stay here,' she insisted. 'Touch nothing.'

I asked her a question that stopped her before she took another step.

'What did you do to get this post?'

She twisted around to look at me.

'You said it was a punishment,' I reminded her. 'And it's clear Sir Cuthbert believes he holds sway over you. He threatened to call the commissioner earlier.' I knew she didn't want me, or probably anyone, to know her past mistakes, but I was more on the backfoot here than I was used to and I wanted to know the type of person I was working with.

'This is a dangerous environment,' I pointed out when she failed to say anything. 'You saved my life earlier, and I owe you for that, but I want to know who it is that I am trusting with my life.'

Her lip twitched. 'You want to know what I am hiding? How about you go first? What's your real name, Jane?'

I accepted her challenge because she was right. My gender preference made no difference to the matter at hand, but I was hiding something too. I dropped my 'Jane' voice.

'My birth certificate says James,' I admitted. 'I am homosexual and prefer to dress as a woman.'

I got a curt nod from the police detective but no opinion or feedback regarding her thoughts on the matter.

'I started a relationship with my boss,' she revealed with

a sigh. 'It went on for several months and I believed he was going to leave his wife to be with me. When she found out, he ended it abruptly. It happened right when he was promoted again and became the commissioner. To get rid of me, on his wife's orders I assume, he sent me here. If you are wondering why I haven't called him out on it and claimed I have been marginalised and unfairly treated, then I guess you don't know how things work in the police. Even if I won such a case, I was knowingly sleeping with a married man and my career would be in the trash either way. I have to make it through my time here, hope he moves on and try to pick my career up afterwards. I did this to myself,' she added as if trying to convince herself it was true.

I resumed speaking in my 'Jane' voice. 'I'm sorry to hear that.' I was at the same time relieved because I had been guessing she was guilty of something far worse than falling for the wrong man.

She gave me a nod of acknowledgement and left me where I was, repeating her instruction to touch nothing.

Left alone, I looked around the room some more. I was way out of my depth and very aware that was how I felt. Usually, I am aware of the need to preserve evidence, but it is not as high on my list as solving the crime and I am always calling the shots. Tonight, I was following the detective inspector around like I was her assistant and beginning to feel quite put out by it.

She left the room, going through a door to the right to explore more of Lord Nugent's chambers and in her absence, I thought about what I had seen so far.

It was a man in a suit. It was Lord Nugent Chamberlain. Eddie said his brother resented him and revealed Lord Nugent lied about being invited to the palace by his younger brother. The elder brother, born without the looks and height of his younger sibling, and without his father's favour, had chosen to remove the thorn in his side. The conjuring of a supernatural creature might seem ridiculous to many, but the Blue Moon Investigation Agency sees this every week.

The police will only investigate for so long before the case finds itself consigned to the unsolved pile. If a death appears to have supernatural causes, you can bet it'll find its way to the cold case file all the sooner.

There was a man behind the murders, and we had the evidence in front of us. Finding it had been easy, and … why was it so easy? The question bonged into my consciousness like a giant bell being rung. Surely, Nugent would have locked his door at the very least? If he wanted to get away with murder, he should have kept all his dragon suit components hidden and never brought them into his private quarters. Why would anyone be so sloppy?

More questions were surfacing, none of which I had answers to.

Yet.

I backed out of the room, making my way into the hallway outside again. I couldn't explain quite what was going through my head at that point, but believing I now knew the identity of the man in the suit, I was going to get his attention and do what the soldiers could not.

I was going to bring the dragon down.

Stalemate

Jogging rather than sprinting, since I had a stitch in my side and was yet to recover my breathing, I left Cassie in Lord Nugent's chambers and made my way back to the stairs.

I heard her calling my name just before I turned a corner. She had undoubtedly come back into the first room we were in and found me gone. If she came into the hallway looking for me, she would find only empty air as I was already out of sight.

It wasn't a deliberate snub. I chose to leave the detective behind because I recognised my plan to be foolhardy and dangerous and because the plan did not require two persons to place themselves in danger.

As I jogged up the stairs to the top floor of the deserted palace, I kept my footsteps light so Cassie might not know which way I had gone. I could hear her calling for me still, her tone becoming exasperated and annoyed. I could also hear the soldiers outside. There had been no shots fired for several minutes but did that mean the dragon had killed Eddie? Or did it mean it had slipped back inside and they couldn't see it anywhere? Had Lord Nugent flown away having completed his murderous task? There was only one way for me to find out.

On the top floor, I tried doors until I found one that was open. The palace is vast, but I felt assured there would be few rooms that had no windows. I needed to make myself as visible as possible both so the dragon would spot me and so the soldiers would see who it was and not shoot me full of holes.

With the lights on to attract attention on the otherwise dark rear façade of the palace, I left the room again and went to find what I needed. Thankfully, I didn't have to look far and due to the soldiers' earlier efforts I even had a rough idea where it would be and how to operate it.

Nerves were making my hands shake and I felt sick from the adrenalin coursing through my body. If there was ever a time to rethink my plan and go home to bed instead then this was it. Of course, like a fool, I pressed on.

There was no parapet running around outside the windows at this level. If I fell out of the window, I was going to die when I hit the ground. I kept that thought in my mind as I threw the windows open and climbed up to stand inside the frame.

'Lord Nugent!' I shouted as loudly as my quaking voice would manage. Then I stilled myself and shouted again, even louder. 'LORD NUGENT! I know it's you.'

In the still air of the night outside, not even a faint breeze dared to ruffle my hair. I couldn't see the soldiers – whether this was a deliberate ploy on their part to stay hidden from the dragon so they could ambush it, or simply because the dark absorbed them at this distance, I could not tell.

I had been able to hear them moving and shouting

orders, the reports reaching my ears from more than one direction until a moment ago. Now they were silent, undoubtedly staring up at the mad, blonde woman framed in the open window.

What the heck was I doing? The question demanded an answer, but when a dark shadow fell across me, and my pulse tripled its speed, I knew it was too late to change my course of action.

I swept my eyes upward to find the dragon silhouetted against the moon. For the first time, I got a good look at my adversary as it stretched its wings to either side. Unable to fathom what I was seeing earlier, it was obvious now that this was no organic creature. It was staying aloft, but its wings were not beating up and down as they would need to. They moved, but far too slowly to keep it in the air. The wings were for show and, if forced to guess, I would say that it achieved flight because there was a propulsion unit fitted into the suit somewhere. The design was ingenious, the work of a seriously intelligent person to not only conceive but to then realise in the flesh as it were.

Now was not, however, the time to be impressed. It was the time to hold my nerve and pray I wasn't throwing my life away on a hunch.

The soldiers were shouting again, and as the dragon started moving, coming straight for me, they opened fire.

The sudden noise made me jump, my nervous legs twitched, and I almost fell from the window when I lost my footing. With just my left hand, I managed to grasp the top of the window frame to pin myself in place.

If I thought my heart was hammering in my chest before, it had been nothing compared to how it felt now. Biting down against rising bile driven into my throat by fear, I sucked in a deep breath and told myself to be ready.

Unlike the soldiers, whose bullets would fly many hundreds of yards, I needed to let the dragon get close to me if I was going to pull off what they could not.

'Jane! What the ...' Cassie's voice ... her exclamation which was then cut short told me not only that she had found me but had instantly worked out what I was attempting to do.

I could hear her running across the room behind me, but I didn't dare turn to look because the dragon was coming right for me.

I held my breath. Truthfully, I was so scared I forgot to breathe. The effect was the same regardless of which way you look at it, but as I waited, and the voice inside my head screamed at me to run away before I became a fireball, I knew it was already too late to escape.

The dragon zipped through the air, a dark shape discernible only because the night sky was brighter with the lights of the city reflecting off the low clouds.

The bright orange eyes seem to mesmerise me, but when I saw the spark of flame appear in its mouth, I snatched my right hand out from where I hid it behind the curtain, and I yanked back on the lever of the fire hose I held.

The dragon was ten yards away and closing fast. If Lord Nugent saw what I was doing and wanted to swerve, I gave him no chance.

The jet of water hit the dragon just south of its face. I hadn't allowed enough for gravity. Nor had I allowed enough for the force of the water. It drove me backward and I lost my balance. Pitching backward, my arms twitched up just as the lance of fire was beginning to form and I doused it in an instant.

I would have fallen from the window at that point had

Cassie not arrived to prop me up. Her assessment of the situation and fast reactions saved me as I was able to hold the improvised water cannon on the dragon.

It should have driven it back or blasted it away. That's what my brain told me. It was hard to see in the dark, but to me it looked as if the water were going right through it and not impacting on the surface.

Screaming in defiance, I held the hose in place, blasting the suit and Lord Nugent. He should have fallen from the sky, but he didn't. The water pressure did succeed in driving the dragon back – it couldn't get any closer to me and each time I saw the fire forming, I hit it again.

Shouts from below – indistinguishable as words – let me know the soldiers were still there and planning something new.

I battled the dragon for twenty seconds or more as it tried to find a way to spew fire at me and I kept pushing it back and dousing the flames. As my arms started to get heavy and my muscles began to cramp from fighting against the backward pressure the jet of water created, I wondered how I was going to overcome the impasse. I couldn't knock Lord Nugent from the sky or make him so heavy from added water that his propulsion unit would no longer keep him airborne, and he couldn't create fire to kill me.

Now that I had tipped my hand and shown I knew who was behind the attacks, he had to kill me and anyone else who might have figured it out. There was a stalemate for now but who was going to tire first?

Me. The answer was going to be me, and I knew it.

A fresh eruption of shooting from below the dragon jolted me. Was I in the line of fire? Were those fools going to hit me instead?

As a fresh reason to be afraid gripped me, I saw the

dragon falter. When I first arrived, Cassie told me that the soldiers' bullets had no effect on the creature. I had seen it first-hand for myself a short while ago when it was chasing Eddie. Now I got to see it close up, but though I could offer no explanation for how Lord Nugent's dragon suit made him impervious – the bullets were not bouncing off as they might if striking armour – something had just happened.

I heard the ping of a ricochet, and the dragon dropped a foot. My stream of water passed harmlessly over its head for a moment until I could adjust my angle once more.

Captain Duncan must have seen it too because I picked up his voice over the din of the water. A second later, the rate of fire increased.

Cassie was swearing and screaming blue murder even as she propped me up. All those bullets were going up into the air and they were going to come down somewhere. Some-where in the middle of London.

So unexpectedly that I almost went forward to chase after it, the dragon disengaged. One moment it had been looking for a way to get to me, the next it was flying away.

I had to drop the hose and cartwheel my arms to stop myself from falling out of the window. Cassie grabbed fist-fuls of my clothing, hauling me backward and into the safety of the room. As I caught my breath, she shut off the hose and the sudden drop in noise – the soldiers had stopped shooting too – was startling.

I turned to thank the detective for saving my life, but she wasn't looking at me. Her eyes were going wide as saucers as she gawped out through the open window in the night.

'Look!' she squealed.

It Doesn't Add Up

The dragon was on fire!

That was what caused Cassie to point and squeal. In the air above the palace, still flying as it headed toward the lake at the far end of the garden, Lord Nugent's flying suit was fast becoming a ball of flame.

Blazing globules of something were leaking from it, falling to the ground below as fizzing fireballs. The dragon flew on and I could no more tear my eyes away from the terrible sight than I could give up drinking tea with my breakfast.

Now easy to see from our elevated position, Cassie and I spotted the soldiers racing after it. Raef was two floors below us on one of the parapets and shouting commands to his troops on the ground. He would follow and they were all to converge and keep firing until it was brought down.

If Cassie was worried about yet more bullets being fired, then she didn't need to be, for the dragon exploded before Raef's troops could start shooting again.

High in the air and visible for miles to anyone looking in

the right direction, the fiery shape blossomed into a fireball all its own. Any hope I held that Lord Nugent might land and survive were gone. I wanted to know why he had concocted this insane plan. To build the suit and be able to fly in it was an incredible feat. Surely, it hadn't just been so he could kill his brother because he got the best of his father's genes?

I watched in rapt horror as the dragon fell from the sky.

'Did it fall into the lake?' I questioned, certain I had seen a splash. It confused me because my brain insisted the fireball had just fizzled out in the water, but there were flames visible in the trees on the far side of the lake. A burning spot on the ground showed where the dragon had impacted.

Cassie grabbed at my arm. 'Come on! We have to go!'

Jerked into motion, I ran after her, abandoning the fire hose where it lay.

The same stairs I ascended earlier led all the way back down to the ground floor. I was out of breath yet again, and about to beg that we slow to a walk because it had to be over half a mile to the lake, when Cassie pointed to a golf cart.

There were two parked side by side to our left.

The seats were damp from the earlier rain, but I was mostly soaked from the firehose water and there was no way the police officer was waiting for me to find a tissue with which I could dry my chair.

In fact, I had to hang on for dear life because Cassie had the cart moving almost before I was in it, and it moved faster than I expected. In two seconds, we were shooting across the courtyard and onto the lawn.

Soldiers, weighed down by their heavy kit, were running

in the same direction but we caught up to them, passed them, and left them in our wake.

Raef, unseen in the dark, shouted for us to come back for him, but Cassie showed no sign that she had even heard him.

We raced on, Cassie's right foot pressed hard to the floor in the little battery-powered cart. The lake loomed ahead of us, growing larger with each passing second.

There were flames ahead to guide us, easy to spot and in the darkness looking innocent - like a bonfire children could be roasting marshmallows over.

The fire was on the far side of the lake, and the water formed a barrier we had no choice but to go around.

When we finally drew near, the flames were beginning to burn out, which was a mercy because I had worried the trees or bushes nearby might have caught fire too.

Cassie let her foot off the pedal, the cart coasting to a stop some five yards shy of the fire.

I could see the dark lump in the middle of the flames. It wasn't moving but then I'd held no hope that the man inside the suit might still be alive.

Cassie climbed down from her seat, approaching the flaming mess slowly and silently. I half expected her to tell me to stay back, but she didn't.

The flames were dying down, the fuel source depleted, and the suit already burnt away. A yard wide strip around the body was singed, the scrubby grass reduced to smouldering ash but there it stopped and would go no farther.

Voices drew my attention back the way we had come. The soldiers had made good time, running across the open ground to get to us and the majority of them were arriving as a pack. There were a few stragglers behind the main body of men, and somehow Raef was at the front.

'Step away from the body,' he commanded, squeezing the words out between gasps for air.

Detective Inspector Munroe didn't even look his way.

'There is a body on the grounds of the palace, Captain Duncan. That makes this a police matter. Unless you think the body still represents some danger to the royal family?' She cast a questioning look at the tall soldier, daring him to argue.

I wasn't really looking at their exchange though. I was looking at the ground.

There was a footprint. There were several footprints. Where the recent rain had softened the earth, the indentations of a man's oxford shoe were leading back to the palace. I spun around to see where they had come from, but the direction they went was the same one the soldiers were coming from.

Troops rushed by me, scuffing up the dirt and ruining any chance I had to investigate.

Captain Duncan, clearly unhappy with the situation, deferred to Cassie and let her claim her right to control the scene. I was certain she hadn't heard the last of the fire upstairs. It was my fault, but I doubted anyone would care about that.

I hustled to draw her attention to the footprints before they were all gone.

'The royals often come out here walking,' she pointed out in a dismissive manner. 'Any footprints you find could be weeks old.'

'They are not,' I argued. 'The rain this evening would have filled them in. These came after the rain and the edges are crisp.'

She wasn't really listening to me, she had two of the

soldiers – they were wearing gloves – attempting to remove the headpiece of the dragon suit. Most of the material on the body was gone, the charred flesh beneath exposed, but the head was formed of something different.

Looking down at it, I observed, 'His body ought to be riddled with bullets.'

Cassie nodded, opting to stay quiet.

'And when I hit him with the fire hose, it should have pushed him away.'

The headpiece came away when one of the soldiers found a clasp under the chin.

'Ma'am?' he asked, checking that they should attempt to slide it off.

The palace detective nodded and the two soldiers, kneeling either side of Lord Nugent's head, carefully eased the black helmet off his head.

His face was burned, but not to the same extent as the rest of his body. It laid to rest any question about who was inside the suit though, for it was Lord Nugent Chamberlain, thirteenth in line to the throne, whose sightless eyes stared up to heaven.

'Sir,' called a voice from the dark, making Captain Duncan lift his chin to see who wanted him.

A cry of anguish caught me by surprise, and I spun around to find Eddie staring at his brother. He was being held back by two of the guardsmen and had Sir Cuthbert at his side. The older man looked weary from the walk across the palace lawn and unable to cope with the gravity of the scene before his eyes.

'Let him through,' commanded Raef.

The handsome younger brother came forward with stumbling steps. Henkel, the little sausage dog, still clasped to his chest. He had escaped his brother on the roof, and I wondered if he had found refuge somewhere or simply evaded the fire when the soldiers drew Nugent's attention with their shots.

There was a whole lot that did not add up, but I wasn't going to get any answers until things had settled down here.

More people were coming from the palace, and looking back across the vast lawn now, I could see the flashing blue lights of multiple police cars parked at the foot of the building.

Fire engines too, a brace of them, here to make sure the fire was truly out, no doubt, were parked to one side. Their flashing lights spun lazily, creating strobe patterns on the rear façade of Buckingham Palace.

Cassie appeared by my side. 'What a mess,' she murmured, though whether the comment was intended for me to hear I could not be sure.

Lord Edward wept for his brother, kneeling next to the body, and sobbing even though Nugent had tried to kill him and was going to be found responsible for the two murders the dragon had already committed.

Had Lord Nugent been trying to get into the palace to kill his brother but failing each time because he was discovered? It fit the events. He killed a soldier in the grounds, and he killed a member of palace staff when he finally got inside. Defeated twice, he then lied about Edward inviting him and was able to get into the palace and bring his dragon suit with him. It was in the abundance of luggage he brought along tonight.

How though was he not shot? The material of the suit was gossamer thin. The propulsion unit, a clunky thing on the back hidden by the wings had burned away to nothing. I was struggling to believe that it could work, propelling him around in the air in such an effortless manner, yet it had. Now there was almost nothing left of it to inspect.

I could accept the ability to fly, but how was he not riddled with bullet holes?

And what about the footprints?

It just wasn't adding up.

Approaching voices drew fresh curses from Cassie. She sighed and muttered several unprintable expletives, turning to face the new arrivals.

'That's my boss,' she let me know.

'The one who sent you here when his wife …'

'That's the one,' she confirmed.

'DI Munroe, report,' a voice commanded, drawing my attention to a man in his fifties. He had an air about him – a sense of power perhaps. In his wake, three men in suits and half a dozen uniformed officers trailed. Cassie's boss was tall and handsome – a lot like Raef in many ways though a good two decades older.

Despite their past, I had the instant impression he was not on her side.

'She set fire to the palace, Commissioner,' reported Sir Cuthbert like a tattletale in school. 'And she brought some fool paranormal investigator into the palace without seeking permission first.'

'I don't need permission to recruit specialists,' Cassie retorted calmly.

I stepped forward, hoping I could shift the blame for the fire away from Cassie.

'Good evening. I'm Jane Butterworth. The fire was my fault.'

'I don't care,' snapped the commissioner, shutting me up

instantly. 'You've no right to be here and any actions you have taken are the responsibility of DI Munroe.'

The commissioner's face bore a severe frown. He looked like a disappointed father as he turned his gaze back to look down at Cassie.

I wanted to argue but I could not think of anything to say that would change the likely outcome.

'Look, I can see where this is going and how badly you want to make me the scapegoat,' Cassie started arguing. 'I did what was necessary and brought an end to the mystery that has been plaguing the palace for the last week.'

'And in so doing caused the death of a member of the royal family!' snapped Sir Cuthbert, his voice dripping with derision.

'He was inside the dragon suit, sir,' Cassie pointed out. 'I think I can safely argue that he caused his own death. He was trying to kill his brother, Lord Edward.'

'I've heard enough.' The commissioner cut her off. 'Get this … woman,' I've been called worse things, 'back to the palace.' He pierced me with his eyes. 'You will sign the official secrets act before you leave tonight, and you will not breathe a word of this to anyone. Do you understand?'

I blinked, giving myself a second of thinking time. 'You wish to gag me so the truth can be hidden?' I was challenging him, and I'll be honest, with a sea of judgemental faces staring back at me, I was feeling almost as scared as I had when I faced down the dragon.

I also felt righteous. What if I refused to sign? I didn't believe they were going to try to make me disappear.

'Please.' The single word, spoken with an imploring voice stopped me in my metaphorical tracks. 'It will break father's heart to hear that Nugent is dead. Please don't burden him with guilt for favouring me over him,' begged Edward.

He was still kneeling next to his brother's corpse, looking wretched and appealing to me for help.

How was I supposed to say no to that?

An hour later, I was in my car and on my way home. The heating was on full, blasting warmth back into my bones. The cold had penetrated right into me, but I was too caught up in events to really pay much attention to it.

Cassie was going to cop the blame for the fire and expected to be fired from the police. It was grossly unfair. When I asked her about fighting it, all I got was a shrug. She could expose her boss and accuse him of sexual misconduct but to drag his name through the dirt meant dragging her own too and that would impact her parents. Even if she won, Cassie didn't believe she would be able to return to active service.

To distract myself, and because there was nothing I could do to help, I had probed her about the holes in the case.

How had Lord Nugent flown? Where were the bullet holes? Why had he been so willing to leave evidence strewn all over his room on the night he planned to kill his brother?

She had no answers and was too distracted by the events shaping her life to give my questions any thought. I felt sorry for her, but there was nothing I could do to help.

When they sat me down to make me sign away my right to ever speak about the events again, I had no resistance left. That was largely down to Eddie/Lord Chamberlain. There was only one Lord Chamberlain now, and whether he liked it or not, he was now the heir to his father's dukedom.

STEVE HIGGS

I flicked my indicator stalk, checked my mirror, and merged with the traffic flowing south out of the capital.

In the morning, I would need to file a report for the business and had no idea what I was going to write. Tempest and Amanda would understand the concept of a gag order – they would just let it go.

I wasn't so sure that I would.

Epilogue

'You see, Henkel? It really was as easy as I said it would be.'
Lord Chamberlain stroked his dachshund's head and down
the little dog's back. Henkel's eyes were closed though he
was not asleep.

The show had gone entirely to plan. Better than he
could have hoped for even. Putting Henkel to one side on
his bed, Edward picked up a jar of moisturising cream from
the dressing table and began to massage some into his
thumbs.

The control rig for the one-off specialist-built drone was
murder on his hands. The hours of practice flights to get
good enough with the controls to be able to make it move
convincingly had left deep welts in his otherwise perfectly
manicured hands. A lifetime of privilege ensured baby soft
skin that rebelled against the sores he now displayed.

It was worth it though. His brother came when called;
Edward extending the olive branch after years of being the
one to shun Nugent. That everyone believed him when he
claimed it was the other way around and then again when

67

he lied to say he hadn't invited Nugent to the palace, well, it just showed that he was the rightful son to succeed his father.

Subduing his brother and carting him across to the lake had been hard, physical work. So too the run back to the palace to operate the dragon again. That paranormal investigator figured things out quicker than he expected, but it didn't matter.

Or did it?

Edward gave himself a few moments to consider the young blonde woman. There was something unsettling about her and he didn't just mean the oversized hands and feet or Adam's apple. He heard her when she questioned Nugent's lack of bullet holes, and while no one else even thought to question the evidence as presented, she found his footprints from carrying Nugent out to the lakeside.

Rigged with an incendiary device and set to go off at the flick of a switch, his unconscious brother burned to death to make everyone think he had been inside the near-weightless drone. They didn't question it, and though they might search the area, he knew they would never find the real drone sunk at the bottom of the lake.

It was a perfect crime, and he was now one step closer to his goal.

As he screwed the lid back onto the moisturiser, he grinned at himself in the mirror.

'One step closer to the throne, Henkel. One step closer. Father will die in a few years' time, and before he does, I need to knock off the eleven people ahead of him. I rather think Prince Markus' wedding might end in the tragic elimination of at least half of them. Imagine it, Henkel.' He swept the dog up and into the air so they were almost nose to nose. 'All those prominent royals in the same place at the same time and then a terrible accident occurs.'

Edward let go of his dog with one hand so he could cover his mouth as he made a big show of gasping at the horrifying concept.

'It's not like anyone will suspect me. I won't suddenly be the king, will I? Not until daddy dearest dies anyway.'

BECKY'S CREATURE

A BLUE MOON INVESTIGATIONS SHORT STORY

STEVE HIGGS

Becky's Creature: Chapter One

The case dropped into my lap four hours ago. A little girl gone missing, snatched from her garden while she was playing. At least that's what the parents said.

Becky Reid is four years old; no age to be away from home. No age to be anywhere except safe with your parents. She wasn't though and no one seemed to have the first clue where she was.

Except me.

The police were at the scene of the abduction when I arrived, their usual surly sneers in place. They don't like me, but I don't get paid to be popular.

My name is Tempest Michaels, and I hunt monsters. I used to be a soldier, but if you think the skill set I developed in that job in any way helps me now, you are sorely mistaken.

So there I was two days ago, hanging around at the edges of the police investigation. I could have gone right through their barrier and made a nuisance of myself – the parents hired me which gave me every right to demand entry. It would have caused friction though, and it's better not to annoy the police.

Besides, I doubted I was going to find anything worthwhile at the house.

Walking a few paces I began my search, finding what I hoped I wouldn't just a few yards from the back garden. I was in an overgrown alleyway that ran between the back gardens of one street and the next.

Something had been through the alley. Something big. The signs were everywhere – thin, twiggy branches snapped by its passing, ground cover plants squished underfoot. Under something anyway.

Caught in a piece of fence was the thing I didn't want to find: a piece of armour. Not the kind of armour a knight wears, more like the kind a creature grows over its organs and squishy bits to protect them.

Tucking it into an evidence bag, not that I would ever submit the item – there would never be a trial for this case – I continued to examine the area. The police picked their way through the alley already, finding Becky's plush bunny where the terrified girl most likely dropped it.

It was how I knew to look there too. I was simply looking with a different set of eyes – ones that knew what to look for.

The police were in the house with the parents where they would establish a bunch of protocols and assure the parents they were doing all that could be done. They would hope for a call from the kidnapper, and they were right to maintain a positive outlook. No call was coming though, and Becky's abductor had no interest in nor need for money.

Leaving them to get on with it, I slid back into my car, a sleek, red Porsche Boxster. I'd spoken to both parents, the conversation conducted over the phone while I was in my kitchen. Becky's mum and dad told me what happened and hired me on the spot.

They expected me to come inside their house, but there wasn't enough time for a face-to-face meeting. Not if they wanted Becky back.

From my office I collected my bag of tricks – things I would need if I was going to survive the encounter. Changing quickly, I donned ripstop trousers, the kind they issue to the military the world over now because they are hardwearing and last forever. Combat style boots covered my feet and a long-sleeved top made from a skin-hugging stretchy fabric coated my torso and arms. A Kevlar vest complete with ballistic protection plates front and back added a layer of safety that would most likely do me no good at all tonight. The final flourish was a pair of fingerless gloves, the kind with Kevlar knuckles.

All in all, it wasn't much, but I would feel exposed without it.

Turning to a tall, steel locker by my office door, I blinked in slight confusion when I took out my charm bracelet, shield talisman, and heavy staff. They were all familiar, right? I'd used them to battle supernatural creatures a thousand times or more, right? So why was there something itching at the back of my head?

Dismissing the sense of unease – Becky could not afford for me to be anything other than one hundred percent focussed, I took out the piece of armour.

It was roughly the diameter of a soda can, but a heck of a lot stronger. The creature that left it behind, whatever the heck it was called, sported thousands of them across its hide. Kind of like an armadillo crossed with a beetle, the ancient evil powering it defied the laws of nature as though it thought them to be entirely optional.

Placing the creature's armour on a mirror, I used my pure silver knife to draw blood from the tip of a finger. Tracking spells are simple things and easy to conjure. I couldn't remember where or when I learned the skill, but my blood provided a link between me and my target, so with a whisper of a spell, "Locatum," I sent my will into the air.

Darkness was beginning to fall outside, the time available to save Becky dwindling with the last rays of the sun. She might have minutes or hours to live but whichever it was, the creature would not let her see morning.

Taking a few precious seconds to lock the door to my office – you would not believe how many times the place has been trashed – I stepped out into the cool air. There was rain about, spots of it coming down with a light breeze. It wasn't enough to dampen the street, but the air held the promise of more convincing weather to come.

Now all I had to do was follow the spell to where it led me and hope the creature's recklessness was born of its youth. The last thing I wanted was to face a mature one. A juvenile I could handle. The bigger ones are too damned fast and near impossible to take down for someone like me.

Becky's Creature: Chapter Two

I knew I was in trouble when I heard the alien bark pierce the night. The rain was starting to pick up and the tracking spell had led me away from civilisation as I feared it would. My boots splashed through puddles, my steps getting faster as I neared the target.

Rochester has its share of unfinished building projects, run down industrial areas, and derelict factories, just like everywhere else, so it was no surprise to find myself close to the waterfront when the power in my spell began to ebb.

I was closing in; not that I had glimpsed the creature yet.

Telling myself I could still be wrong – the bark did not sound like that of a juvenile - I readied my shield and pushed will into my heavy staff. From deep inside the old wood, a deep purple light faintly glowed, showing here and there where I'd carved protective runes into the surface.

However, when I heard Becky scream, the terror the little girl felt dripping from the shrill sound bouncing off the abandoned buildings all around me, I threw all caution to the wind. Maybe I was rushing toward my own death. Maybe there was nothing I could do. I was sure as heck going to find out though.

Drawing extra juice into my body where I held the magical energy ready to dispense, I rounded a corner. I was moving fast, but not so fast I wouldn't be able to react if what I found there was ready for me.

Mercifully, it wasn't, but that was the only good news. The creature I knew I would find had a surprise for me.

It wasn't alone.

There were two of them, both fully grown adults. They turned toward me as I skidded into the clearing they dominated. The river flowed to their rear; dark and dangerous, but perhaps also tactically helpful.

Their chitinous bodies reflected the moonlight where the rain made their armour slick and shiny. Rising to stand on their back feet, they had short fore limbs a bit like a dinosaur, though not so short as a T-Rex, and powerful back legs. Their digits ended in dull claws, but I wasn't fooled into thinking they couldn't rip me to shreds with them if they got close enough.

Their heads, like chunks of granite with tiny black eyes set deep between plates of armour, zeroed in on the human form a little more than half their size and weight.

Casting my eyes a few feet lower, I saw that I was matched against a mated pair – there was, um, well one of them had something between its hindlegs and the other did not. Becky was probably being taken to feed their young – the very thought made my stomach revolt.

"Ok, Tempest, what now?" I asked myself, readying fire to launch with my staff, but unwilling to do so until I saw Becky.

The situation called for something less dangerous I

decided, whipping out a tendril of energy that coiled around my right fist.

They couldn't both have the girl, and as soon as they moved, I saw it was the female who hid Becky's tiny form in her giant shadow. Target identified, I unleashed my spell against the male.

Designed to create a concussive wave, the spell's energy dissipated against the creature's chest, bowling it backward. It was an excellent first volley, but they knew to be wary now and I wouldn't get a second shot in so easily.

With Creature One tumbling still, I brought my attention to bear on the female. She had Becky and that was going to make fighting her tricky. I couldn't risk hurting the little girl, but getting myself killed before Becky had a chance to get away was pointless, so I had to do something.

Readying fire, I threw a wall of it, aiming to the female creature's right. If she chose to run, she could escape to her left, taking Becky and leaving me to fight her mate.

However, the creature stepped away from the fire. She was mad now and not about to be cowed by a feeble mortal – a species they thought of as prey. With a bellow she charged, head down and all four limbs powering the terrifying beast across the ground.

Just as I hoped.

The almost insignificant form of Becky Reid lay on the wet concrete in the creature's wake. Now, with the creature finally separated from the little girl I came here to rescue, I could unleash my arsenal.

The trick with these creatures is to find the weak spot.

Able to chance unleashing some raw power without frying Becky, I sucked in a lungful of rainwater moistened air and gave the creature everything I could muster. Conjuring fire and then manipulating it is relatively easy, I guess. However, if you wanted me to explain the intricacies of the spell at that precise moment, I would have struggled, so let's just stick with 'I made fire'.

The lance of fire, white hot and concentrated into a thin jet sprang forth with enough heat that I could feel it crisping the fine hairs on the back of my hand. It would cut through steel or rock if given a few seconds to take effect.

The creature acted as though it were an annoying tickle. Ducking a shoulder as it ran, it met my fire with the thick armour plates on its back. Like hitting a mirror, they bounced off. Shooting across the open space, the fire spread, losing its intensity.

Shutting it off, for the creature would be on me in a few seconds, the only indication that I hit it at all was a slight glow on its shoulder.

Yeah, the trick with these creatures is to find the weak spot. The problem is that they don't have one.

That's why I turned and ran. Rain filled my vision, running off my hair and into my eyes even as the heavy droplets stung my face, but I didn't need to go far.

Derelict industrial areas might make great places for monsters to hide, but they are also the best places for someone like me to fight them because I can do as much damage as I like.

Knowing I couldn't outrun it, I choose to slow it down.

Manipulating magnetic fields with a spell I'd devised all myself, I tore from the ground old rails from a long since disused train track. Bending them up as I passed, I created barriers the creature was forced to swerve.

They weren't going to save me or Becky, but I was just warming up. Reaching the wall of an old factory, I turned to face the oncoming threat. Some fifty yards beyond it, the first creature was back on its feet and heading toward Becky.

I couldn't deal with them both at the same time, but if I could halve the number of opponents, I might stand a chance.

Few creatures like fire. Very few. But fire can be deflected, and their armoured hides would protect them long enough to kill me if I employed it.

Electricity though. Well, that's a different story and I just happened to notice there was power coming to the pylon above my head.

Gritting my teeth, I kicked over an old wooden pallet that lay at an angle against the wall and stepped onto it.

The female ran between the twisted steel rails where they jutted from the ground and just before it hit the centre, I directed all my effort into the high tensile steel cable twenty yards above my head.

This was a dangerous tactic to say the least. I was next to an asbestos building – the prevalence of its use probably one of the reasons the area had been abandoned – and I could climb if I needed to. Hopefully though, the shock would earth through the ground and not spread too far in each direction.

If it did, I wasn't entirely convinced the wood of the pallet would be enough to keep me safe. Too late to change my mind, I loosed the spell, sending it skyward through my staff where it crackled and fizzed angrily. As though the magic were alive and hungry, it sought out the cables,

Unlike my attempt to slice the creature into pieces, this time the lance of fire cut right through the cable in an instant, and I held my breath as the severed ends fell.

Time stood still, the nightmare scenario taking forever to play out. Prescribing an arc, the longer piece of cable swung lazily down, a fat, white spark bridging the remaining distance when it was still more than a foot from the ground.

It followed the path of the rainwater running from the cable, the world turning white in the next instant. Now, I didn't get shocked, but standing atop the pallet, I could feel all the hair on my arms standing on end and when my vision cleared a moment later, there was steam rising from my clothes and skin.

Above my head sparks continued to fall, twinkling pinpricks of violent white light cascading from the condenser pot mounted on the pylon like a trapped firework searching for escape.

In the next second, it exploded, drenching the area in another burst of incandescent brightness that robbed my night vision as the light faded away to leave a sickly layer of inky black.

My breathing came in deep gasps, the terror of my situation overwhelming me. I needed to get off the pallet. I needed to go. There was still another of the awful beasts to fight, but did I dare step down to the ground?

Becky got me moving.

The fragile form of the little girl was back on her feet, her hands bunched into the trailing hem of the summer dress her mother picked out this morning. I was too far away to see if she was crying, but I knew she would be; the salty droplets mixing with the rain that refused to stop falling.

The male creature I bowled over right at the start of our fight had come to a stop, staring at the smoking, broken form of its mate. I hoped to God my panic-fuelled attempt to kill one with electricity worked. Otherwise, it was going to wake up at some point and would probably not be in a good mood.

Leaping from the wooden pallet, my lead foot splashed into an inch-deep puddle, but the shockwave of electrical current I feared was mercifully absent. Drenched, feeling weary from the adrenalin and the draw of energy each spell took from me, I pelted across the concrete apron as the creature snatched Becky before she could hope to escape.

Yet again, I couldn't hope to launch an attack without risking Becky's life, however the creature had no interest in fighting me. To my great surprise, it turned and ran.

I blinked, my running footsteps faltering while my brain struggled with what it was seeing. I got to do that for about half a second before the little girl screamed again. This time it wasn't just a cry of fear though.

She said, "Help me!" With the driving rain beating on the ground around me like a million tiny drums, it was hard to hear her little voice. I hadn't imagined it though.

Angling my feet to intercept the creature, I cut a diagonal toward the river. Could it swim? Did I want to find out? What would I do if it dove into the water? I didn't want to think about it, and as it happened, I didn't get to because a new player entered the field.

Running one second, I was twisting and fighting an invisible force the next. Something touched me; I felt a hand on my shoulder that made me twitch violently. I broke away, jolting from the unexpected shock of it.

Spinning to face back the way I came, I glared at the empty concrete plateau. There was no one there and that could only mean one thing: I was dealing with a powerful practitioner. I'd never been able to achieve spectral displacement – the ability to touch and handle objects or people remote from one's location.

Expecting a blow to land and unsure what I could do to protect myself from it, I tried to relax so I could roll when it came. When three or four seconds passed and nothing happened, I snarled against my fear and started running again.

The creature was going to get to the river before me though only because I had been distracted. Unable to shift the unease creeping down my spine, I told myself to concentrate even though I felt certain the invisible force could attack again at any moment.

Worse yet, a pessimistic little voice inside my head wanted me to know the likely ability level of the practitioner hiding somewhere in the shadows behind me, meant it was entirely possible they would simply snuff out my life before I even knew they had thrown a spell.

Since I could do nothing about it, I raced across the wet ground focused solely on trying to save a little girl. Was the magician to my rear something to do with the two creatures I came here to fight?

Questions, Tempest, always with the questions. Focus on the task at hand. Becky has no one but you.

As predicted, the creature reached the edge of the concrete a few seconds before me, but it didn't dive into the black abyss of the river. Instead, it skirted the building nearest the water and carried on running.

Becky's Creature: Chapter Three

Between the building's outer wall and the edge of the concrete where it plunged a couple of yards to the water below, the detritus-riddled path could be no greater than a yard and half wide. The creature's bulky shoulders took up more than two thirds of the available space as it careened through discarded shopping trolleys, old pallets, and what was clearly the rear axle from a Ford Capri.

Leaving a shopping trolley in its wake, buckled and wobbling on a suicidal path for the water, the creature barrelled onward.

Built like an ankylosaurus, nature never intended the thing I chased to move with speed, so even on four legs it wasn't going to be able to outrun me. It did, however, have a lead and I was beginning to tire.

Slowed by the weight of my Kevlar vest, and the rain which soaked my clothes, I was keeping pace with the beast when I ought to be able to catch it. In fact, it didn't seem to matter how hard I ran, I just couldn't close the gap.

"Tempest!" A strange yet familiar voice invaded my consciousness.

Was that the new player calling to me? Was it someone I knew? They hadn't followed their original interruption with an attack as I expected, but whoever they were and what-ever they wanted was entirely secondary to saving the little Becky.

Becky clung to the creature, pinned to its chest and cradled by its left front limb. Her face peered at me, eyes locking with mine over the creature's shoulder. There was no way I was going to let her down.

What could I do though? I couldn't catch the creature, it was fast enough to stay ahead of me, or maybe that should be I was too slow to close the gap. I also couldn't use magic. Even at such close quarters where I might reasonably be able to select an aiming mark well away from Becky, there was still the risk the creature would tumble into the river taking her with it.

That left me one option, and it wasn't one I liked.

I might not be able to catch it on foot, but I could throw. In a perfect world, this would be where I yanked a magical bola from my belt or conjured one from thin air. I could swing it above my head and launch it at the creature's legs with at least a semi realistic chance of tripping it.

With no such weapon in my arsenal, I went with the only thing I had: my staff.

Roughly two yards long and weighing about forty pounds, it's been employed as a cudgel more than once with predictable results. Hefting it with my right hand, I took aim, accepted I had no idea what I was doing and went with the million to one shot I hoped might take out the creature's back legs.

Like a miracle occurring before my eyes, the staff

caught between its knees and with the creature's next steps, it tripped. The staff banged against one leg, ricocheting back to hamper the other and with its centre of gravity continuing forward without legs to support it, the nightmarish monster toppled.

Becky screamed, but the poor little girl had been doing so much of that I was barely aware of it any longer.

"Tempest!"

I spasmed at the sound, twisting to see where it came from even as I ran to get to Becky. The voice had resounded inside my skull without feeling the need to observe basic manners and go through my ears.

Then the hands on me again, a strange sensation against which I fought to wriggle free. Slipping through them, I was filled with horror to see the creature slam into the ground. The hand holding Becky was thrust out in front, a fleeting mercy, for though she avoided being crushed, the creature's hand popped open with the impact.

The four-year-old bounced clear, but in the absolute wrong direction. Running as hard as I was, I could see I wouldn't make it to her before she went over the edge and into the water.

Could she swim? Would she float? If I dived in to save her, would the creature follow us both?

I ran, fighting to make myself move faster, but all I could do was watch as she vanished from sight with a final squeal.

The creature was already getting up when I leapt over it, my staff trapped somewhere under its body. Without it, I was close to defenceless, but my thoughts were not on my own survival, but on the little girl who drew me here.

Skidding to a stop, I planned to tear off my boots and Kevlar vest at the very least before diving into the frigid water below. I knew it was warm enough to be survivable, but that didn't mean it wouldn't suck my breath away.

"Tempest!"

This time I ignored the voice completely. Not because I knew I could, but because Becky hadn't fallen into the water after all. She clung to an outcropping of wood, the remains of what must once have been a jetty. Just above the water, if she reached up and I lay flat on the surface, I felt sure I could reach her.

Hopeful eyes met mine when she looked up imploringly.

She was safe for now. Probably as safe as she'd been since I arrived. If I could just defeat the creature or drive it back, Becky might stand a chance.

Swinging my body around, I pushed a whisper of will into my defensive shield, the barrier of pure magical energy thrumming into life before me. Anchored to a charm bracelet my grandfather left me, I could position and control the shield with my wrist.

The creature charged, causing me to set my feet and ready myself. A yard away it dropped its shoulder to smash into my barrier. If it had enough juice the thing might shunt me clear off the side and into the water, so I dropped the shield at the last possible second and sidestepped neatly to leave clean air in the space my body once occupied. Don't ask me where the idea came from; it was one of those spur of the moment things.

I got to see the creature's eyes go wide when it turned its head toward me and flailed a clawed limb that almost snagged my arm. Unable to reverse its forward trajectory or correct its inertia, the creature flew over Becky's head and into the murky wave with a mighty splash.

Not wanting to trust my eyes, I gulped in badly needed air and watched for it to surface. Would the current carry it downstream? How deep was it here? They built and launched warships from the royal dockyard a few miles downriver; it was deep there, but this close to shore, was the creature about to wade out and resume the fight?

Nothing happened for several heartbeats, but I had to force myself to move even when I allowed myself to believe the fight was over.

Tearing my eyes away from the water, I lowered myself to the ground, lying in a puddle - not that I could get any wetter.

Reaching down, I said, "I've got you, Becky. Let's get you back to your mum and dad."

Our fingertips touched, but the gap was just a few inches too far. Bringing my arm back so I wouldn't topple, I shimmied forward to the point where I knew I would fall if I went any further and tried again.

I was going to be able to grab her hand this time and Becky looked to weigh so little I would be able to pluck her to safety with no bother at all.

Our hands met, her digits tiny in mine.

Just as my hand closed around hers, the river erupted, the creature's head bursting from the surface not a yard behind the little girl.

I yanked, but the creature got to her with both fore-limbs, stripping her from my grip as I stared into her terror-frilled eyes.

"BECKY!"

Shunted from one state of reality into another, I blinked in confusion at my new surroundings.

"Good, Lord, man. What were you dreaming about?"

Amanda knelt on the bed next to me, looking down at where I was now propped on my elbows.

My skin felt cold where I was sweating, not where rain

ran over it. Cool air coming from the window caused goose-bumps to rise. I wasn't in a derelict industrial area and there were no monsters to fight.

Relieved it was just a dream, I sank back into my pillow.

"You okay, hotshot?" Amanda asked. "Am I safe to go back to sleep?"

I nodded but noticed for the first time that my girl-friend's thin t-shirt was stretched somewhat invitingly over her chest where the cool air from the window was making two rather interesting points.

Amanda saw the wolfish grin beginning to form and tracked my eyes.

"Not a chance, mister. You're all sweaty for a start. The bedclothes will need to go in the wash in the morning." To accentuate her point, Amanda returned to her side of the bed, wrapping herself in the covers and turning her back so she faced the other way.

Disappointed, though not in the least surprised, I turned my gaze to the book resting on my nightstand. Promising I would refrain from reading urban fantasy stories before bed, I took the book, some nonsense about a German wizard, and dropped it unceremoniously into my sock drawer.

Settling down to sleep, I wondered if I might find myself back at the river's edge when sleep found me again.

I was just drifting off when the voice stole into my dream once more, the tone this time lacking patience and filled with unspoken threat.

"Who's Becky?"

vinci-books.com/shadow-mine

This case is like nothing Tempest has ever faced before, and just maybe this time, the creature is real.

Called to investigate a mystery at a local gypsum mine, paranormal detective, Tempest Michaels, expects to find a rational explanation for the strange events... instead, he discovers a body and horrified staff. Recent earthworks exposed something ancient, twisted, and above all evil. It has claimed one life already and the staff are terrified for who might be next. No one saw what it was though, just a glimpse of a shadow.

Turn the page for a free preview...

Shadow in the Mine: Chapter One

THE SHADOW

Tuesday, October 10th 2156hrs

Have you ever had that sensation when you are certain someone is watching you? I think we all get it from time to time. It's an old defence mechanism hardwired into the back of our brains, and it kept humans alive when there were things around that would hunt us.

When we look, twitching our heads around sharply to check for danger, there is usually no one there, or there is someone there and it turns out to be the cute girl or boy from the office that you have been secretly crushing on for months. They have spotted you watching them and have developed a mutual interest – you hope.

But what if when you look there is no one in sight, but your brain continues to insist you are still being watched? What if something that isn't really anything then moves, withdrawing farther into the shadows?

'Did you see that?' asked Wayne, squinting into the darkness.

Wearing ear protectors to stop noise getting in, and because it was jolly cold and they kept his ears warm, Owen didn't hear anything.

When Wayne thumped his shoulder, it made him juggle and slop over half of his freshly made tea.

'What?' he demanded angrily, pulling the right side of his ear protection back so he could hear his partner's response.

'There's something over there,' Wayne nodded his head, speaking up so Owen would hear.

'Yes,' Owen agreed. 'It's a mine.'

They were at the entrance to B face, waiting to be assigned tasks by their charge hand, Gary. Gary was a decent sort, advancing to lead the crew through the basic equation of being older and knowing more.

Fletchers' gypsum mine had been open for almost two years but had been beset with problems since the start. Safety issues was the most recent concern. Machinery was breaking down even though it was all quite new. A lifting rig snapped just a few weeks ago, sending tons of rock crashing down to the ground where it almost killed three workers. Since then, they had the Health and Safety Executive breathing down their necks. Every shift they were reminded to obey all the safety regulations - as if any of them were daft enough to disobey the rules.

The owners, a father and son team, blamed the recent run of accidents on the residents of a nearby village. There was nothing in any direction apart from that one small settlement just a couple of miles from the entrance to the mine's land.

The locals hadn't said a word when the mine was proposed or when it opened. However, about a year ago, they started making all kinds of noise, protesting and campaigning. The owners believed they were responsible for sabotaging the mine equipment.

Some staff had already quit, taking jobs at other mines even though it meant traveling farther each day. Wayne had no interest in changing jobs – the Fletcher's mine was a convenient driving distance and paid well enough. Even if there was something untoward going on with the locals, he felt confident it would blow over.

'You can't halt progress,' he muttered, still squinting into the dark.

Owen had his ear defenders back on already and was trying to drink what was left of his tea before Gary arrived. Their shift started in a few minutes.

'Hey, there's something out there!' insisted Wayne when the shadow he'd been staring at moved. He shot out an arm to point to it, knocking Owen's arm again just as he was about to take a swig.

Owen replied with a question about the legitimacy of Wayne's parentage.

Wayne heard the insult, but it didn't really register. He'd seen something for sure the second time. It was moving in the shrubland beyond the light cast by the mine's overhead lights. There were wild deer here – they saw them occasionally, but that wasn't what he had seen.

It was only there for a second, popping up as if it needed to check the lay of the land before vanishing again. Whatever it was, it had long spindly limbs. As nightmare creatures surfaced in his imagination, Wayne did his best to quash them.

'It was probably a tree,' he told himself out loud. 'Yes, a tree moving, and the way the clouds were shifting cast a shadow just when I looked at it. It looked like something but

...' Wayne looked up at the cloudless sky and swallowed down hard on his rising uneasiness.

Cursing himself for watching too many late-night horror movies – it wasn't his fault, that's what's on at that time of the day and his body clock was all messed up from working nights – he squinted into the darkness again.

'Alright, let's have everyone's attention,' called Gary, wandering out to face the assembled men with a clipboard in his hands. 'Here are tonight's assignments.'

Gary looked up, making sure his team was listening. Faces were looking back at him. All except one.

'Hey, Wayne!' He whistled loudly, putting two fingers in his mouth to create a high-pitched noise.

Owen had one half of his ear defenders off again so he could hear what Gary was going to say. When he looked to see why Gary was shouting and whistling to get Wayne's attention, Owen took great pleasure in jabbing an elbow into his partner's ribs.

Wayne made an 'Ooof' noise as he gasped an unexpected breath.

'Whenever you're ready,' Gary mocked him, nodding his thanks to Owen.

Wayne, rubbing the sore spot under his left arm, listened to what Gary had to say but could not help twitching his eyes across to see if the shadow had reappeared.

Shadow in the Mine: Chapter Two

RIGHT TO ROAM

Friday, October 13th 1117hrs

I stared into the strangely shaped hole and said nothing. The mine owners were standing behind me, waiting to hear what I had to say. They were two peas in a pod, both sporting beer bellies that jiggled when they walked, both wearing the same clothes even though it wasn't a uniform, and both displaying the same haircut though the father's was going rapidly grey.

They were an inch taller than me which made them just over six feet and quite ordinary looking. They were the kind of men you pass in the street but never notice.

They made the call the previous evening and I promised to visit this morning. I'd been looking into a gargoyle case at a stately home, but we were having a slow week, so Amanda, my girlfriend and business partner, who was working the case with me, carried on alone so I could tackle what sounded like a meatier investigation.

It was meatier. To start with, I had a dead body, not just some petty thefts which I felt sure were going to be down to the staff who worked at the stately home. They were the ones claiming to have seen gargoyles moving about inside the house.

The body was that of a mine worker called Wayne Calder. He'd failed to report in after his shift three days ago. According to Stefan Fletcher, the elder of the father and son pair, his absence went unnoticed until the next shift came in and someone pointed out that his timecard was still live.

A complete search of the one hundred and twenty square mile property failed to reveal his whereabouts. When they couldn't raise him at home or anywhere else, and calls to his parents, ex-wife with whom he had three children, and even the landlord at his local public house, all came back with the same result – "We haven't seen or heard from him" - they called the police.

A further day went by before his body was found and that was where it all started getting creepy.

Wayne's body was desiccated, sucked dry of all moisture and his corpse was completely mangled. I hadn't seen the body, nor read a coroner's report, but I was willing to take Stefan Fletcher's word for it. Worse yet, he was found by other mineworkers in open ground not far from the current edge they were cutting.

They called it a mine, but to my way of thinking, a mine is something underground. This was on the surface or, at least, mostly on the surface.

Anyway, Wayne Calder reappeared, very dead, very dry, and in a place men had been walking only hours before. Someone took him away, sucked out his juices, and put him back.

The killer wanted his victim to be found.

It was macabre. And that, of course, is why they called me.

My name is Tempest Michaels. I am the owner of a paranormal investigations agency which I started after I left the army. It pays the bills.

The hole the Fletchers wanted me to look at was not where Wayne Calder was found. It was inside a cut – what they call the leading face of the open mine. The workers found it the day before Wayne went missing. I couldn't help but stare at it. There were footprints leading away from it, but not man-made ones. Nor were they from any animal on the planet. They were sort of domelike, with a teardrop shape, the point of which was at the back if I was viewing them correctly.

Someone had gone to some effort to set this up.

'What do you think, Mr Michaels?' asked Stefan Fletcher, prompting me to speak because I had been silent for so long.

I thought someone was playing an elaborate trick but had learned long ago that I cannot simply state there is nothing paranormal going on. Doing so either gets me thrown off the case – hard to make money that way. Or it starts a big argument between the believers and the told-you-soers. Sometimes that argument can rage for days, and it never creates anything productive.

Turning away from the hole, I said, 'It's far too early to draw any conclusions, gentlemen.'

'But you are going to take the case, yes?' asked Stefan.

His son frowned, and for the first time I noticed how annoyed he looked.

'We don't need him, Dad,' Colin Fletcher insisted. 'He's just some charlatan preying on people's superstitions.'

I gave him credit for looking me in the eye when he insulted me.

Stefan came to my defence before I could consider what I might like my response to be.

'No, son, he's the real deal. I've read all about him and he came highly recommended.'

'We can't afford him,' argued Colin, changing tactics. 'We are bleeding money, Dad, and with the workers on strike until we can ensure their safety, we shouldn't be spending anything unless we absolutely have to.' Colin was agitated, his hands and feet twitching as if he was feeling nervous and wanted to be somewhere else.

The older man closed the distance to his son, placing a fatherly hand on his shoulder when he said, 'This is necessary, boy. Mr Michaels is an expert in cases like this. He'll find the culprit and get us working again far quicker than the police. That's what we need and if it costs us a few quid, that's the price we have to pay.'

It was clear his son was not convinced and wasn't going to be no matter what his father said. Colin glared over his father's shoulder at me, unashamed of his opinion, but silent for now.

Pivoting around to face me again, Stefan asked his question again.

'Will you take the case, Mr Michaels?'

I could hear the sense of hope in his voice. The hole appeared during one of the weekly maintenance shut down periods. Typically, the mine operates twenty-four hours a day, seven days a week, but to perform routine maintenance there was a two-hour shut down every third day. I guess it was that or suffer a much longer shut down when something critical broke.

Apparently, the hole caused some speculation when it

was discovered, but the miners' interest in it was only passing – they had quotas to achieve.

When Wayne's body was found they took a closer look at it and called a strike within hours. On top of the safety issues and several near misses that could have been fatal, the loss of one of their own proved too much.

The hole wasn't just a hole, you see. Rather, it was a pocket in the gypsum. A pocket which had contained something vaguely humanoid, and which appeared to have been burst open from the inside.

Something inside had decided to get out and the day after they found the strange hole on one face of their open mine, a man vanished.

I couldn't blame Stefan for wanting to hire me.

A light drizzle began, coming from the east and threatening to bring more rain with it.

I shrugged my shoulders to force the collar of my coat up closer to the skin of my neck. Too often during my time in the army I had been an accepting, yet unwilling victim of the elements. Back then I had no option but to put up with it and tough it out. Now I could go inside if I felt so inclined.

I drew in a deep breath and held it for a prolonged second before letting it go. It was all the thinking time I required. There were scared people, the local police assigned to figure out what happened to poor Mr Calder were most likely stumped by the circumstances of his demise, and there was very definitely something spooky going on.

It was a trademark case for me, and I knew I would choose to investigate it even if they were not offering to pay me to do what I love. There was someone behind this. Someone with ill intent and devious purpose.

Now I just needed to figure who, why, and how.

The radio in the Fletchers' utility vehicle burst into life.

'Boss, this is Angus. She's at it again!'

Having no idea who 'she' might be, or what the 'it' was that she was apparently doing again, I watched the two mine owners to see how they reacted.

Mostly they said bad words. The kind of words my mother automatically crosses herself after hearing if she is in public even though she will employ them herself if she drops a plate or stubs her toe.

Stefan crossed back to the cab of his utility vehicle, leaning through the open window to snatch up the handset.

'Where is she?' he growled.

His son, Colin, was already climbing into the passenger's seat as his father got his answer, the two of them leaving me where I stood to deal with this latest issue. As if suddenly remembering me, Stefan jerked a thumb at the back seat of their truck.

'You'd better come along, Mr Michaels. Sorry, we have to deal with this, but it won't take a moment, and we'll take you back to the office straight after.'

I had no intention of letting them go without me – it was over a mile back to my car for a start and that was across churned up, muddy ground. I haven't exactly gone soft since I left the army, but if I don't have to get mud all up my legs and ruin my shoes, I won't.

Also, whoever the mystery lady was, she had the owners instantly hot under the collar and that intrigued me. The hole in the ground was interesting, the desiccated and butchered body of Wayne Calder unexplained, yet I was certain I was going to find a person or persons behind the crime, so checking out who this mystery person was and what they were up to had become an obvious next step.

I got a last look at the hole as the senior Mr Fletcher spun the truck around and roared off over the scrubland surrounding the open mine.

'Who is the 'she' you are racing to intercept?' I enquired.

Stefan swore again. 'Mildred Marchant. She's the head of the local ramblers' society.'

That single piece of information coloured the picture in nicely.

Staring between the front seats to look out through the windscreen, I said, 'Let me guess. They are arguing right of way through the land you now own and are continually breaking through your fence lines to enter areas that are not safe to cross.'

'Bang on,' replied Stefan. 'This is the fourth time this week. They haven't walked this land in decades and wouldn't have either if we didn't erect fences to keep them all safe. It's a mine for crying out loud. If they fell into it or got run over by one of the gypsum trucks after cutting our fence, you can bet they would try to blame us.'

'It's ridiculous,' commented Colin, his voice a low growl.

The Fletchers were not happy, and I understood their standpoint – I would be unhappy too if it were my problem. I offered no opinion, acknowledging that I knew too little about the different sides of the argument to speak my mind. However, I had met with several deliberately awkward people in my time – my mother was one of them – and could see the likelihood that Mildred was just being difficult because she could.

As we bounced across the uneven ground, low scrubby bushes all around but nothing growing higher than a couple of feet, it was easy to make out a gaggle of people in the distance. Stefan adjusted his trajectory to meet them head on and continued to grumble and swear until, skidding to a stop a few yards from them, he jumped out and started shouting.

'Don't mind him,' instructed a woman in the middle of the group. 'Just carry on. We have every right to be here.'

I could have guessed the speaker was the infamous Mildred Marchant, but Stefan confirmed it.

'Mildred, we have talked about this. It isn't safe for you to be here.' Stefan was doing his absolute best to keep his cool. 'The police are already on their way.'

'We have every right to roam, Mr Fletcher!' she snapped in his face. 'Even if that does upset your profit churning money machine as it strips the earth of its natural resources.'

The group of ramblers had ground to a halt and were looking about uncertainly.

'Perhaps we should go back, Mildred,' suggested a woman in an orange waterproof coat. She looked to be in her fifties and not all that enthralled to be out in the elements. The sky threatened rain.

'Nonsense, Rosie,' spat Mildred, clearly uninterested in anyone else's opinion.

'But he said the police are coming,' Rosie pointed out, voicing her concern while glaring at the back of Mildred's head.

Mildred smiled as if it were amusing. 'We are not committing a crime. We are the locals here and we have the right to roam.'

'But you do not have the right to cut my fences!' snarled Stefan. 'That's four times this week.'

'Stop erecting fences then!' shouted Mildred, going red in the face.

'It's for your own safety!' screamed Stefan in response.

His chest was puffing out and his hands were clenching and unclenching. 'Maybe I should just let you roam, Mildred. Be my guest and walk where you will on my land. Then maybe we'll see what happens to you!'

Worried his father might be about to strike the barmy old bat, Colin grabbed hold of his dad's arm and tugged him away.

'The police are here, Dad,' Colin nodded his head across the scrubland and when I looked, I too could see a four by four with a light bar on its roof heading our way.

Mildred, a smugly satisfied smile on her face, retreated a few yards to stand with her party of reluctant ramblers.

There were muttered conversations I could not hear, but they all fell silent when the police off-road vehicle parked, and a local police officer got out.

He was wearing a uniform and no badge of rank which made him a constable. In his late thirties, I felt that made him old to still be on the bottom rung, but perhaps he was late to join the service. Carrying a few extra pounds around his middle and a trim, yet convincing black beard, the Caribbean man looked unhappy.

'This is the fourth time this week,' the police officer pointed out.

Exasperated, Stefan gawped. 'What are you telling me for? Arrest her, can't you? This is getting ridiculous.'

'We have discussed this Stefan,' the officer replied in a bored tone. 'The law is clear, and they have a right to roam. You can appeal but as you already know, it will take a year or more to get a decision.'

'He threatened to kill me,' shouted Mildred, sounding pleased with herself. 'I have witnesses.'

'What?' Stefan's face took on a surprised and guilty expression. 'I never threatened you.'

'Yes, you did,' Mildred came forward, wagging her finger at the mine owner as she closed the distance between her and the police officer. 'You invited me to wander your land and told everyone I would find out what would happen to me if I did. You don't want to pay to put in safe paths for us, so you are going to kill me instead.'

Stefan protested. 'That is not what I said!'

I'll be honest and admit that I lost interest at about this point. The cop met my gaze and rolled his eyes when he thought no one else was looking. I wanted to talk to the local police - they would have pictures of Wayne Calder and an autopsy report, but that wasn't going to happen right now.

I checked my phone, finding a text message from Amanda, and turned away to answer it while the argument about rights to roam raged on.

When they were finally done, Colin led his dad back to their truck as the ramblers carried on their merry way.

The local cop had given them a warning to steer clear of the mine and a sterner warning to the Fletchers to put gates or styles in their fence line, accept they could do nothing about the ramblers, and to carve out safe paths with warning signs to prevent anyone accidentally falling into the mine.

Stefan's knuckles were white as his grip attempted to crush the life out of his steering wheel on the way back to their office, but whatever thoughts were going around in his head, he kept them to himself.

My piqued curiosity to see the people breaking through his fences had waned. I expected to find the murder victim had been killed by a fellow mineworker but was open to find my first guess proved wrong. Whatever had happened to Wayne Calder it was not at the hands of Mildred or any of her ramblers – they looked like they were fresh from Sunday School.

Grab your copy...
vinci-books.com/shadow-mine